This month, in

HER LONE STAR PROTECTOR
by Peggy Moreland,

meet Robert Cole—private investigator and drop-dead-gorgeous bachelor. Rob was on a mission to solve a murder, but instead he found himself falling for Rebecca Todman—his lovely young suspect!

SILHOUETTE DESIRE
IS PROUD TO PRESENT THE

TEXAS
Cattleman's Club
The Last Bachelor

Five wealthy Texas bachelors—all members of the state's most exclusive club—set out to uncover the traitor in their midst... and find true love.

* * *

And don't miss
TALL, DARK...AND FRAMED?
by Cathleen Galitz,
the third installment of the
Texas Cattleman's Club: The Last Bachelor series,
available next month in Silhouette Desire!

Dear Reader,

Celebrate the rites of spring with six new passionate, powerful and provocative love stories from Silhouette Desire!

Reader favorite Anne Marie Winston's *Billionaire Bachelors: Stone*, our March MAN OF THE MONTH, is a classic marriage-of-convenience story, in which an overpowering attraction threatens a platonic arrangement. And don't miss the third title in Desire's glamorous in-line continuity DYNASTIES: THE CONNELLYS, *The Sheikh Takes a Bride* by Caroline Cross, as sparks fly between a sexy-as-sin sheikh and a feisty princess.

In *Wild About a Texan* by Jan Hudson, the heroine falls for a playboy millionaire with a dark secret. *Her Lone Star Protector* by Peggy Moreland continues the TEXAS CATTLEMAN'S CLUB: THE LAST BACHELOR series, as an unlikely love blossoms between a florist and a jaded private eye.

A night of passion produces major complications for a doctor and the social worker now carrying his child in *Dr. Destiny*, the final title in Kristi Gold's miniseries MARRYING AN M.D. And an ex-marine who discovers he's heir to a royal throne must choose between his kingdom and the woman he loves in Kathryn Jensen's *The Secret Prince*.

Kick back, relax and treat yourself to all six of these sexy new Desire romances!

Enjoy!

Joan Marlow Golan

Joan Marlow Golan
Senior Editor, Silhouette Desire

Please address questions and book requests to:
Silhouette Reader Service
U.S.: 3010 Walden Ave., P.O. Box 1325, Buffalo, NY 14269
Canadian: P.O. Box 609, Fort Erie, Ont. L2A 5X3

Her Lone Star Protector
PEGGY MORELAND

Published by Silhouette Books
America's Publisher of Contemporary Romance

Special thanks and acknowledgment are given to
Peggy Moreland for her contribution to the
TEXAS CATTLEMAN'S CLUB: THE LAST BACHELOR series.

This book is dedicated to W. J. and Carmen Ann Fisher. Thanks for all
the free advice on goat raising, cattle breeding, fence building,
brush clearing, snake dodging, poison ivy cures and heavy-equipment
driving lessons. We're in your debt…just don't ask us to pay up!

 SILHOUETTE BOOKS

ISBN 0-373-76426-X

HER LONE STAR PROTECTOR

Visit Silhouette at www.eHarlequin.com

Printed in U.S.A.

PEGGY MORELAND

published her first romance with Silhouette in 1989 and continues to delight readers with stories set in her home state of Texas. Winner of the National Readers' Choice Award, a nominee for the *Romantic Times* Reviewer's Choice Award and a finalist for the prestigious RITA Award, Peggy has appeared on the *USA Today* and Waldenbooks bestseller lists. When not writing, she enjoys spending time at the farm riding her quarter horse, Lo-Jump. She, her husband and three children make their home in Round Rock, Texas. You may write to Peggy at P.O. Box 2453, Round Rock, TX 78680-2453, or e-mail her care of eHarlequin.com.

"What's Happening in Royal?"

NEWS FLASH, March—There's a murderer loose in Royal, Texas! Sources report that the death of Eric Chambers was no accident—someone wanted Wescott Oil's vice president of accounting out of the way for good. But who? The police don't have any leads at the moment. Luckily, Royal's own sexy sleuth, Robert Cole, is on the case!

Our sources have been trying to talk to Rebecca Todman, the attractive florist who discovered the murder—but it seems Rob has beaten us to the punch! He's been spending an awful lot of time with Rebecca…and are smoldering glances and searing kisses part of his new interrogation procedures? If so, we predict Robert will have suspects lining up at his door for questioning.…

First theft and now murder—things have gone from bad to worse at Wescott Oil. Our reporters tried to get hold of Sebastian Wescott, but the CEO has refused to comment on the proceedings. Could Sebastian be hiding something? While nobody seems to know for certain, rumors are flying, and his friends at the Texas Cattleman's Club seem worried.…

One

Rebecca glanced down at the clipboard she'd propped on the console of her minivan and worried her lip as she did some quick math. Ten, fifteen minutes tops at Eric Chambers's house to water and tend his plants, another fifteen at the Olsens' to do the same. Ten or less at the Mortons' to deliver the new potted palm Mrs. Morton had purchased for her sunroom. Factor in driving time of about twenty minutes and she should make it to her shop, In Bloom, in time to open for business by 9:00 a.m.

But barely, she reflected with a frown as she pulled to a stop in front of Eric's house. Her frown deepened to one of puzzlement when she noticed Eric's car parked on the drive. Strictly regimented about every aspect of his life, Eric always left for work precisely at 7:30, which allowed her to tend his plants undisturbed, an arrangement they'd made from the get-go that had suited them both.

Wondering if perhaps he was ill, she gathered the tote filled with her supplies and headed for the back door. Though he had given her a key to his home when he'd hired her to care for his plants, she opted to knock, rather than let herself in as she normally did. She didn't want to catch him unawares…or worse, in his underwear. She choked a laugh as she waited, imagining the expression on the face of the very prim and proper Eric Chambers if she were to catch him dressed in only his B.V.D.'s.

Her smile faded when her knock produced no response. With a harried glance at her wristwatch, she rapped her knuckles on the door again, louder this time, then pressed her ear to the wood, listening, but she didn't hear a sound from inside. Convinced that Eric was indeed ill and possibly too sick to get out of bed, she tried the doorknob. To her surprise, it turned in her hand.

She hesitated a moment, unsure whether she should just barge in. With another glance at her watch, she pushed the door open and stepped inside. Though the kitchen was immaculate as always and flooded with cheerful morning sunshine that streamed through the breakfast-room windows, goose flesh popped up on her arms. The house was quiet. Almost *too* quiet.

"Eric?" she called uneasily. She tiptoed toward the doorway that led to the hallway and his bedroom beyond. "Eric?" she called again, raising her voice.

When she didn't hear a reply, she waited uncertainly, wondering if she should go to his bedroom and check on him or just tend his plants and leave.

"He's your neighbor," she scolded herself under her

breath, ''and he lives alone. The least you can do is see if he needs anything, especially since he's been so kind to send customers your way.''

Silently berating herself for her selfish ingratitude, she marched toward the bedroom door. She paused at the open doorway, sent up a silent prayer that he was decently covered, then peeked inside. The room was empty, the bed neatly made. A suit coat was draped with meticulous care over a valet stand near the closet. Certain that she would have found Eric in bed, delirious from a raging fever, she glanced toward the partially open bathroom door.

He had car trouble, she told herself, and turned back for the hall. Probably caught a ride with someone from his office. Promising herself that she would call Wescott Oil and check on him the minute she arrived at her shop, she filled her watering can at the kitchen sink and hurried through the house, watering the potted plants and checking for signs of disease as she nipped off the occasional dead bloom and withering leaf. When she had completed her duties, she returned to the kitchen and rinsed out her watering can, anxious to be on her way.

But he could have had a heart attack, her conscience scolded as she tucked the watering can back into its slot in her tote. *Or a stroke! You can't leave without first making certain he isn't home. You'd never forgive yourself, if you find out later that he was lying on the bathroom floor, praying someone would find him.*

Rebecca groaned, wishing her conscience—as well as her overactive imagination—would, just this once, take a holiday. She was running late enough, as it was. She headed for the back door.

But you can't leave! Not until you make sure he isn't here!

She stopped at her conscience's frantic urging, her hand on the knob. *But I've been in every room of his house,* she argued silently. *He's not home!*

You didn't look in the bathroom, the stubborn little voice reminded her.

Rebecca glanced over her shoulder at the hallway and the bedroom beyond. Knowing her conscience was right, that she wouldn't be able to live with herself if Eric was indeed lying unconscious on the bathroom floor, she dropped her tote onto the counter and trudged down the hall. She passed through his bedroom, the deeply piled carpet muffling her steps, and nudged open the partially closed bathroom door. "Eric?" she called as she stepped inside.

Rebecca stumbled back, her eyes widening in horror, her hand flying to her mouth to smother the scream that clawed its way up her throat. Eric was slumped on the closed toilet seat, dressed in crisply pleated black slacks and a starched white shirt, his hands, bound by a black belt, lying slack between his knees. A dark silk tie with a burgundy paisley print was tied nooselike around his neck and secured to the towel rack above the commode. His eyes were open, staring, his mouth slack, his skin a deathly chalk-white, his features distorted by an unnatural swelling.

Numbed by the sight, Rebecca stared, knowing without moving any closer that Eric was dead. She knew what death looked like. She had seen it firsthand on her husband's face, even applauded it, knowing that with his death, she was at last free of him. She gulped, staring, as memories flashed through her mind, blurring Eric's features, until it was her husband's face she stared at. Blood had spurted from the gash on his forehead when the impact of the automobile crash had thrust him forward, his chest hitting the steering wheel and his head slamming against the windshield. The gurgling sounds of his last breaths screamed through her mind.

She squeezed her eyes shut, remembering the anger that had twisted her husband's handsome features prior to the crash, the fear for her own life that had gripped her when he'd forced her into the car with him.

The scream that had risen to her throat when she'd first entered Eric's bathroom burned higher and higher, pushing against her tightly pressed fingers. Wheeling, she ran blindly for the kitchen. She yanked the phone from its base and frantically punched in 9-1-1. One ring buzzed in her ear before her knees gave way beneath her and she sank weakly to the floor, her fingers trembling as she clutched the phone to her ear.

"This is the 9-1-1 operator. May I help you?"

"Yes," Rebecca sobbed, the single word scraping like a razor over her raw throat. She pressed her hand over her mouth to hold the emotion back. "He—he's dead," she managed to choke out.

"Who's dead?"

"Er-Eric." She gulped and turned her head to stare at the hallway, picturing again Eric's face. His unseeing eyes. "Eric Chambers," she murmured, the image slowly changing, the face becoming that of her husband's, the unseeing eyes the eyes of the man who had made her years as his wife a holy hell. She banded her fingers around her forehead and squeezed her eyes shut, not wanting to remember...and knowing she would never forget.

Mornings were usually quiet at the Texas Cattleman's Club. But on this particular morning, there was a different quality to the silence. A heaviness. A somberness. Yet the air seemed to hold an electrical charge, as well. A sense of expectancy crackled through the club. One of impatience. A need for action.

A murder had been committed in Royal, the victim an employee of a member of the Texas Cattleman's Club, and what affected one club member affected them all.

Though usually empty at that time of day, the club's cigar lounge was almost filled to capacity, with members having dragged the heavy leather chairs into huddled groups of four and eight. The members' conversations were low, hushed, as they reviewed the facts of the case and speculated on the identity of the murderer.

In a far corner of the room Sebastian Wescott sat with a group of his closest and most trusted friends. William Bradford, CFO and partner in Wescott Oil Enterprises. Keith Owens, owner of a computer software firm. Dorian Brady, Sebastian's half brother and an employee of Wescott Oil. CIA agent Jason Windover. And Rob Cole, private investigator.

Though all the men were included in the conversation, it was Rob and Jason whose expertise Sebastian sought in finding Eric Chambers's murderer.

Sebastian glanced at Jason. "I know that your participation in this case will have to remain unofficial, due to your status as a CIA agent, but I'd appreciate any assistance or advice you have to offer."

Jason tightened his lips and nodded. "You know I'll do everything I can."

Seb turned to Rob Cole. "The police, of course, are conducting their own investigation, but I want you on the case. I've already informed the police that they are to coordinate their efforts with yours.''

Rob nodded, his mind moving automatically into investigative mode. ''Brief me on what you know about the murder.''

Seb dragged a weary hand down his face, but didn't come close to smoothing away the deep lines of tension that creased it. ''Not much.''

''Who found the body?''

''Rebecca Todman. New in town. A neighbor of Eric's. She owns a floral shop and, according to her, was hired by him to tend his plants.''

Rob frowned as he studied Seb. ''You don't believe her story?''

Seb shot to his feet, tossing up a hand. ''Hell, I don't know who or what to believe!'' He paced away a few steps, then stopped and rammed his hands into his pockets. He heaved a breath, then glanced back at Rob. ''Sorry,'' he muttered. ''I haven't had more than three straight hours of sleep in the past week, and when I arrived back at the office this morning, I had *this* dumped on me. The only thing I know for sure is that Eric is dead. And I want his murderer found.''

''Okay,'' Rob agreed, aware of the responsibility Seb assumed for all his employees. ''Let's start at the beginning and review the facts.''

Seb sat back down, more in control now, but a far cry from calm. ''According to the police reports, the Todman woman found Eric this morning around eight o'clock when she went to water his plants. He'd been strangled with his own necktie.''

Rob leaned forward, bracing his elbows on his knees. ''Any sign of a break-in?''

''No.''

"Robbery?"

"Not that the police have been able to determine."

"Any known enemies?"

"None that I'm aware of."

"How about women? Any disgruntled girlfriends in his past? A jealous husband maybe looking to get even?"

Seb lifted a brow. "Eric?" At Rob's nod, he snorted. "Hardly. I don't think Eric's ever had a girlfriend. Lived with his mother until she died a couple of years ago. The only woman in Eric's life is—was," he clarified, frowning, "a cat. Sadie. Treated her like she was human. Rushed home from work at lunch every day, just to check on her." He shook his head. "No. Eric didn't have any jealous husbands gunning for him, and he didn't have any girlfriends, either. Just old Sadie."

"What about this Todman woman?" Rob pressed. "Do you think she and Eric could have been involved?"

Seb lifted a shoulder. "Maybe. Though I doubt it. Eric was…well, he was a bit on the strange side. A loner who kept to himself. Very protective of his personal life. No," he said, his frown deepening as he considered. "More like secretive. Forget it," he said, waving away Rob's suggestion of a possible relationship. "There was nothing between them. He was a lot older than her. And he was fussy, if you get what I mean. About the way he dressed. The way he kept his house and car. Lived his whole life on a time schedule, never deviating a minute or two one way or the other. Hell, a woman would have messed up his life too much for him to ever want one around. The guy was a confirmed bachelor."

"Sounds like about 90 percent of the members of the Texas Cattleman's Club."

Seb cut Rob a curious glance, then leaned back in his chair, chuckling. "Yeah, it does. Though that number's dwindling fast. I'm beginning to wonder how we're going to decide how to fund the profits from the Texas Cattleman's Ball."

Jason leaned forward, interjecting himself into the conversation. "I thought the terms of the bet were that the last bachelor standing prior to the Ball got to choose which charity would receive the money?"

"True," Seb conceded. "But since Will here is married now and out of the running, that only leaves four of us. Just makes me wonder how many more will fall before time for the Ball."

Rob rose, preparing to leave. "You can quit your worrying, because there'll be at least one." At Seb's questioning look, he tapped a finger against his chest. "Me."

After leaving Seb, Rob dropped by the police department and read the report the investigating officers had filed, requested a copy for his own files, then drove to the florist shop to question its owner, Rebecca Todman. He parked his sports car across the street from the shop, unfolded his long legs from the cramped interior and climbed out, slamming the door behind him. With his gaze on the shop, mentally assessing the place, he pressed a thumb against the security device attached to his key ring, activating the car alarm, then slipped the keys into his pocket and strode across the street.

A bell chimed musically above his head as he stepped inside. The heavy floral scent of fresh-cut flowers immediately sent his sensory nerves into overload. He wrinkled his nose and sniffed once to clear his sinuses before beginning a slow inspection of the shop and its occupants.

He pegged the owner immediately. A slim woman, about five foot six, short, dark blond hair, wearing a bright yellow bib-style apron with In Bloom embroidered in a colorful garland of flowers across its front. Though serviceable, the apron didn't stand a prayer of hiding the feminine curves beneath it. Small, firm breasts, slender waist, delicately shaped rear, long, shapely legs. On another occasion, Rob might have taken the time to weave a few erotic fantasies of having those legs wrapped around his waist.

But not today. And not about this woman. Until he proved otherwise, Rebecca Todman was a suspect.

And Rob never complicated a case by becoming physically involved with a woman he'd been hired to investigate.

From his vantage point in the center of the shop, he had a good view of her standing in front of a glass-fronted refrigerator. She was sorting through a tall bucket full of long-stemmed roses while another woman—obviously a picky customer—watched, alternately nodding her approval or shaking her head at the stems selected. Though he pretended to browse, he kept a careful eye on the two, hoping to get a feel for the owner's current emotional state before approaching her.

Though she appeared calm to the eye, keeping a patient smile in place for her customer, Rob easily detected the level of nerves beneath. She was scared…or, at the very least, shaken. Her face was pale with high points of color on each cheek, and her hands trembled slightly, causing the petals on the roses to quiver.

She glanced his way and inclined her head slightly,

inviting him to browse. He nodded and pretended to do so while she arranged the roses in a vase, attached a ribbon and card, then walked her customer to the door.

When the bell chimed, signaling the customer's departure, she headed his way, her smile still in place, though he could see the strain beneath it.

"Welcome to In Bloom. May I help you find something?" she asked politely.

He set down the potted plant he had been examining and glanced her way. "Maybe." He pulled his wallet from his back pocket and flipped it open, exposing his private-investigator license. "Rob Cole," he said by way of introduction, while watching her face for a reaction. "I've been hired by Wescott Oil to investigate the death of Eric Chambers."

He watched her face drain of what color still remained there. She took a step back, bringing her hands together at her waist to wring. "I've already told the police all I know."

He nodded. "Yes, ma'am. I read the report. But I was hoping that you wouldn't mind answering a few more questions."

She turned and moved behind the counter. "Like what?" she asked uneasily as she picked up a daisy to add to a fishbowl arrangement she'd obviously been working on earlier. He noticed that the tremble in her fingers was stronger now, the pallor of her skin a ghostlier white.

"Just a few questions about your association with Eric Chambers. Were you friends?"

Her chin quivered, but she quickly pressed her lips together to still it. "I'd like to think we were. We were neighbors, plus he was a client."

Though Seb had mentioned the business association,

Rob wanted to hear Rebecca's explanation. "Client? He was a customer in your store?"

She chose a cluster of pink snapdragons to add to the arrangement. "That, too, but he also contracted with me to take care of his houseplants. Eric liked having live plants in his home, but didn't have the time or talent to tend them."

A huge white cat jumped up onto the table where Rebecca worked, startling Rob. It arched, rubbing its back along her arm, and meowed pitifully. Rebecca's chin quivered again.

"Hey, Sadie," she murmured, and set aside the flowers she was arranging to draw the cat into her arms. She nuzzled her cheek against the cat's fur. "Are you missing Eric, sweetheart?"

Rob immediately tensed. "Eric? That's Chambers's cat?"

She nodded, then set the animal down, giving its sleek head one last, sympathetic stroke. "He was very attached to her, and her to him. I couldn't very well leave her in the house alone, not with Eric...well, not without anyone there at the house to feed and look after her any longer."

"Eric didn't have family?"

She shrugged her shoulders and went back to arranging the flowers. "None that I know of."

"So you just took the cat?"

She snapped up her head, the lift of her chin defensive. "I didn't steal her," she said evenly, "if that's what you're thinking. The police know that I have her. I'm just taking care of her until they can locate Eric's next of kin."

Rob offered her what he hoped came across as an apologetic smile—though it mattered little to him, whether he had insulted her or not. He wanted information and would get it, no matter whose feelings he stepped on along the way. "I didn't mean to imply that you had stolen the cat. But I am curious about Eric's family."

The tension eased a bit from her shoulders and she turned the fishbowl around to place flowers on the opposite side. "As I said, I'm not aware of any family. He was an only child and lived with his mother until her death a couple of years ago. But that was long before I moved here," she added as she slipped a sunflower among the other blooms.

"Any girlfriends that you know of?"

Her gaze went to the cat, who sat on the edge of her worktable, cleaning her paws, and a ghost of a smile touched her lips. "No. Just Sadie."

"Male friends?"

She cut her gaze to his, her blue eyes flat with resentment. "If you are asking me if Eric was gay, I don't know. We never discussed his sexual preferences."

So, he'd made her angry, Rob thought. Good. People usually revealed more in anger than when they were in control. "What *did* you discuss, then?"

She snatched at a length of yellow ribbon hanging from a row of colorful spools at her right, cut a strip, then slipped it around the lip of the fishbowl. Though he could tell she resented his prying, she didn't allow her anger to affect her work. The bow she tied was soft, flowing and free of the tension obvious in her shoulders and hands.

"The weather. Plans for a cutting garden in his backyard he wanted me to design. General things. Nothing personal," she added, slanting him a look before turning the fishbowl to inspect the finished arrangement.

Rob followed her gaze. Thick wedges of orange and lemon slices filled the base of the clear glass bowl and helped hold the flower stems in place, as well as adding a unique decorative touch to the arrangement. He nodded his head toward her creation. "Clever idea."

She pressed her lips together, stubbornly refusing to accept his comment as a compliment. "It isn't mine. I saw a similar arrangement done with limes and expanded on it."

"Still a clever idea."

She picked up the arrangement and turned her back on him to place it in the glass-fronted refrigerator behind her. "Do you have any other questions, Mr. Cole? As you can see, I'm rather busy."

He lifted a brow at her curt, dismissive tone, a sharp contrast to her earlier politeness. "Just one. Are those flowers for sale?"

The question caught her off guard, which is what he'd intended, and she glanced back over her shoulder to peer at him. "You mean this?" she asked, indicating the arrangement she'd just placed in the refrigerator. At his nod, she stammered, "Well, y-yes. It is."

He pulled out his wallet and tossed a credit card on the counter. "I'll take it."

Rebecca strained to peer out the window, watching as he pulled away from the curb. When she could no longer see him, she sank weakly down onto her stool.

A private investigator? she asked herself.

He looked the type...although she wasn't completely sure what a private investigator was supposed to look like. But he certainly appeared tough enough for the job, if that was a requirement. Broad shouldered. Slim hipped. A face that looked as if it had been carved from stone. She shivered, remembering.

He hadn't cracked a smile the entire time he'd been in her shop. Not that she had smiled, either. But she hadn't particularly felt like smiling. Not after the chilling morning she'd just experienced. Finding Eric's murdered body. Having questions hurled at her by a detective from the police department faster than she could even think. Then to have to relive it all for another investigator, this one hired by Wescott Oil, Eric's employer.

Sighing, she pushed to her feet and began to straighten her worktable, not wanting to think about the incident any longer. With a neatness born from habit, she put away her scissors and snips, straightened the rolls of ribbon, then brushed the bits of soil and fallen petals from the table and onto her open palm. As she stooped to dump the trash into the container below the table, she caught a glimpse of a black sports car through the front glass window, driving by her shop.

She straightened slowly, recognizing the car as Rob Cole's. What was he doing? she wondered, then felt a jolt when her gaze met his. She stared, unable to look away. Blue, she thought, and slicked her suddenly dry lips. His eyes were blue. The same deep shade as the morning glories that climbed her back fence. Though he wore sunglasses now that prevented her from seeing the color, she remembered.

How could she ever forget?

Late that same night, Rob sat before his desk in his home office, the room dark but for the glow of his computer screen. After several hours of painstaking research through government records stored on the Internet he'd pieced together the life of Rebecca Todman prior to her move to Royal, Texas. Twenty-seven-year-old female. Widowed. Former address Dallas, Texas. Housewife. No priors. Not so much as a traffic ticket to blot her record. The woman was squeaky clean.

With a groan, he let his head fall back and scrubbed his hands over his face. So why did he have the feeling that Rebecca Todman was hiding something?

"Because my gut tells me she is," he muttered under his breath.

Knowing that his gut was seldom wrong, he dropped his hands to the keyboard and quickly typed information into a search engine. He tapped his fingers against the mouse while he waited for the results to appear. Spotting a listing from the archives of a Dallas newspaper, he clicked the link, then narrowed his eyes as he studied the article and accompanying photo that came into view.

Rebecca Todman? he asked himself, frowning at the woman pictured at a local charity event. Her hair was longer in the picture than her current style and her manner of dress much more sophisticated, not to mention more expensive, than the serviceable khaki slacks, pastel blouse and apron that he'd seen her wearing at her shop. So why the drastic change in appearance? he asked himself. A disguise? A mood swing?

No matter what the reason, he told himself, the change in appearance only intensified his gut feeling that the woman was hiding something. And his gut was rarely wrong.

And, at the moment, empty.

Remembering that he hadn't eaten anything since breakfast, he pushed back his chair. In the kitchen he dug around in the refrigerator until he found a box of take-out fried chicken. He lifted the lid and sniffed, trying to remember when he'd put it there. With a shrug, he tossed the box onto the breakfast bar and dragged up a stool. He plucked out a thigh and took a bite, narrowing his eyes as he chewed, thinking over his interview with Rebecca Todman and his first impressions of the woman.

Scared...or, at the very least, rattled, he amended. Guilty? He shook his head, then took another bite. For some reason that assessment didn't quite fit, in spite of her drastic change in appearance prior to moving to Royal. She didn't look like a murderer. She looked more like... What? he asked himself, frowning as he tried to profile her. A librarian? A Sunday school teacher? She had an innocence about her, a polite and gentle manner of speaking and moving that would qualify her for both.

Physically she didn't look capable of doing another person in. Overpowering Eric Chambers and strangling him with his own necktie had required a strength he doubted she possessed.

Or did she? he reflected further, thinking of the kind of muscle work a shop like hers would require. Some of those potted plants he'd seen were large, and for the most part she worked alone, a fact he'd already verified. Which meant she would have to be stronger than she appeared, in order to lift them. But strong enough to overpower a grown man?

Grabbing a chicken leg from the box, he strode back to his office and flipped on the overhead light. He crossed to his desk and pushed through the papers littering it, until he found the item he wanted. Tossing the half-eaten chicken leg into the trash can, he held up the picture of Eric Chambers, taken from the employee files at Wescott Oil. Five foot seven or five foot eight at the most, Rob figured, examining the photo closely. Approximately 140 pounds. A small man. And, from what Rob could tell, one who hadn't spent any time at the gym. If caught off guard, it was possible that Rebecca could have overpowered Chambers.

He puffed his cheeks and dropped onto his chair again, tossing the picture aside. So why was he having such a hard time believing Rebecca Todman murdered Eric?

Thinking better with paper and pen in hand, he plucked a pad from his desk and reared back in his chair. With his bare feet propped beside his monitor, he began to jot down questions. When he'd finished, he returned to the first item he'd listed and studied it.

Motive? He tapped the end of the pen against his lips as he mentally listed the possibilities, focusing on the two behind most murders committed: money and revenge. Was Rebecca Todman in desperate need of money? Desperate enough to kill to acquire it? He made a quick note to check into her finances, then began to jot down reasons she might want revenge. Romance gone sour? Business deal gone bad? Feud between neighbors?

He tossed down the pen in disgust, his instincts telling him none of the reasons jibed. But maybe there wasn't a reason. Maybe Rebecca Todman was simply a psychopathic killer, a man hater, who had considered Chambers an easy mark and killed the guy just to get her jollies. He rolled his eyes and picked up his pen again, going back to the first item he'd listed under revenge: romance gone sour.

Rob picked up the picture of Chambers, took one look and tossed it aside with a snort. No way. The guy had no physically redeeming qualities and, if what Rob had heard was right, was a loner and probably a mama's boy.

Rebecca on the other hand, he reflected, scooping up a picture taken of her unawares at the crime scene, was young and attractive, and had a kind and generous heart, a trait exemplified by her willingness to take in Chambers's orphaned cat. He arched a brow, studying the photo, noting the soft roundness of her breasts outlined behind the light cotton pastel blouse and the feminine curve of hip beneath the khaki slacks…and found himself wishing for a bed and a couple of hours of hot, sweaty sex with the woman.

Swearing, he dropped the picture to the desk and rose from his chair, dragging a hand over his hair as he headed for the door. *You're tired,* he told himself. *Or horny. Maybe both. Otherwise you wouldn't be having sexual fantasies about a woman you suspect is guilty of murder.*

But one thing was for sure. Horny or not, he'd be talking to Rebecca Todman again. Until he'd proved to himself otherwise, she was still his prime—and only—suspect.

Two

Rob snatched his cell phone from its holder on his sports car's console. "Rob Cole."

"I've done some checking and here's what I've got."

He whipped the car to the shoulder of the road, wanting to give his full attention to the call. Earlier that morning he'd phoned Chuck Endicott, a private investigator from Dallas with whom he shared information from time to time, and requested that Chuck track down what he could on Rebecca Todman. "Shoot," he said, picking up a pen to jot down notes.

"In a nutshell, her in-laws hate her. Think she was responsible for their son's death. They tried to make a case of it, but the police couldn't find enough evidence to even fill out a warrant for her arrest."

"Did you check it out?" Rob asked, frowning.

"Yeah. The guy bought it in a car wreck. He was driving. Lost control of the car and broadsided a bridge embankment. Driver's side. The wife walked away with only minor scrapes and bruises.''

"Any signs of foul play?"

"The car was totaled, but the in-laws demanded an inspection, accusing the daughter-in-law of tampering with the brakes or steering. Results came back negative.''

Rob's frown deepened. Two deaths in which Rebecca Todman was either directly or indirectly involved. Coincidence? "What's your take on this?"

"Me? I'd say the in-laws are screwballs, with a grudge to grind. Kinda reminds me of my old lady's folks.''

Rob snorted a laugh. "I'll be sure and share the comparison with Leah.''

"Man! Don't go telling my old lady anything. I stay in the doghouse enough, as it is.''

"Deserved, I'm sure,'' Rob replied dryly. He glanced at his watch. "Listen, Chuck. I gotta go. Thanks for the help, buddy. I owe you one.''

Rob carefully timed his arrival at Rebecca's shop. He wanted to catch her alone, and he figured the best way to do that was to show up as she was closing for the day. At three minutes until five, he stepped inside the shop and glanced around, but didn't see any sign of her. "Ms. Todman?" he called, thinking she might be in the storage room behind the counter. When she didn't reply, he rounded the counter and peeked through the partially open door. Though the overhead light was on, the room was empty.

Frowning, he turned and took a second look around. The only other door was a glass one that connected to an adjoining greenhouse. Rob headed that way. He found the temperature inside the greenhouse to be warmer than that in the shop and a hundred times more humid. Perspiration immediately beaded on his forehead and upper lip.

"Ms. Todman?" he called again. He didn't hear a response, but that didn't surprise him. Fans installed along the walls and on the ceiling made enough racket to drown out any other sounds. He started down an aisle framed by long wooden tables covered with pots of flowers and greenery of every size, shape and description. He finally caught sight of her at the far end of the greenhouse. She was standing with her back to him before a table scooping potting soil from a large bucket and depositing it into compartmented trays.

When he was close enough, he laid a hand on her shoulder. "Ms. Todman?"

With a startled cry she dropped the shovel and ducked away, throwing an arm over her head, as if to ward off a blow.

A hole opened in Rob's stomach, spilling in a sickening acid as he stared at her, unable to move. He was familiar with that reaction, that instinctive response for self-protection. But he hadn't intended to frighten her when he'd approached her, nor did he have any intention of hurting her. Hell, he'd barely even touched her! He'd wanted only to get her attention, to warn her of his presence, so that he *wouldn't* frighten her.

But obviously he'd failed, judging by her cowering response. Not wanting to frighten her more than he already had, he hunkered down to peer up at her. "Ms. Todman," he said quietly. "I didn't mean to startle you. I just dropped by to ask you a couple more questions."

Slowly she lowered her arm until her gaze met his.

She quickly turned away…but not before he caught a glimpse of the raw fear in her eyes.

She combed shaky fingers through her cropped hair. "I'm sorry," she murmured, unable to look at him. "You caught me off guard. I thought… I thought I was alone."

He rose as she picked up her shovel, and noted that her hand was shaking. "I yelled, but I guess you didn't hear me over the sound of the fans."

She nodded, but kept her head down, her gaze on her work.

He moved to stand beside her and scowled when her hand bobbled, spilling potting soil across the table. Obviously, being alone in the shop with him made her uncomfortable, a condition that would, he suspected, affect her willingness and accuracy in answering the questions he had for her. He glanced at his watch. "It's closing time, isn't it?"

"Yes."

"How about if we go down the street to the Royal Diner and talk? I'll buy you a cup of coffee. It's the least I can do," he added, "after scaring a couple of years off your life."

"I've already told you everything I know."

He bit down on his frustration. "I thought you said you were Eric's friend. Don't you want to see his murderer put behind bars?"

"Of course I do," she replied impatiently as she swept the spilled soil onto her palm and dumped it back into the bucket. "It's just that I don't know what else I can possibly tell you."

"You might be surprised. Talking with me could trigger something in your mind. Something that seemed unimportant to you at the time, but might possibly be important to the case.''

She wavered uncertainly, her forehead pleating in indecision. Then her shoulders sagged in defeat. ''All right,'' she said as she slid the shovel into the rack attached to the side of the table. ''Just give me a minute to lock up.'' Turning away from him, she wiped her hands across the seat of her slacks, managing to avoid his gaze and keep a safe distance as she made her way back down the aisle to the front of her shop.

Rob stared after her, watching her hands move across that delectably shaped tush. *A murderer?* he asked himself as he started after her. If she was, she was one hell of an actress.

And *he* was definitely horny, he decided with a frown. Otherwise, why would he find it so difficult to tear his gaze from her rear end?

Rob sat opposite Rebecca in a booth, watching as she nervously shredded a napkin she'd plucked from the dispenser at the end of the table. Not once during the walk to the diner had she made eye contact with him. And though he'd tried making idle conversation, he'd finally given up, frustrated by her monosyllabic replies.

Determined to resolve the question of her innocence, he braced his forearms on the table and leaned forward. ''I know you're probably anxious to get home, so let's get this over with. Was the morning you found Eric the first time you'd been to his house?''

Her fingers closed around the shredded napkin, balling it within her fist. ''No. I've been caring for his plants for a couple of months.''

''The morning you found him, was the house locked when you arrived?''

"No."

"Was that unusual?"

"Yes. Normally he would already have left for work by the time I arrived."

"Did you know, prior to entering the house, that Eric was at home?"

"I thought he might be. His car was still in the driveway."

"Yet you entered anyway."

"I knocked first. When he didn't answer, I tried the door and found it unlocked."

"Since you're in his house on a regular basis, I assume that you would notice if anything was out of place."

"Yes, but nothing appeared out of the ordinary." Her eyes rounded as if she'd just remembered something. She laid her hand on the table and leaned forward, her expression hopeful. "It did seem unnaturally quiet, though."

His investigative instincts sharpened. "How so?"

"The radio. Usually it's playing. Eric always listens to the weather and traffic reports while he eats his breakfast, then leaves it on to keep Sadie company while he's away. Is that important?"

"If the coroner hadn't already established an approximate time of death, it might be." He lifted his hands. "As it is, it's just another detail to add to the file."

She drew her hand from the table, looking downcast. "Oh."

"The report stated that you found him in the bathroom."

She squeezed her eyes shut and nodded, as if haunted by the scene. Was it an act? he wondered.

"Yes. He...he was on the toilet seat. A necktie was

wrapped around his neck.'' She lifted her hands as if to demonstrate, then, with a shudder, dropped them to her lap.

"Did you attempt to resuscitate or touch the body in any way?"

She shook her head. "No. I knew he was dead. His face was white and his—" She gulped, tried again. "His...his features were distorted. Swollen. His eyes open and staring."

A choked sound had Rob glancing to his left, where their waitress stood, a coffeepot in hand. Laura Edwards, he remembered from other visits to the diner. Her stricken look surprised him, but he attributed her reaction to her having overheard Rebecca's rather graphic description of Eric's body.

She shoved the pot toward them. "C-coffee?"

Rob turned over the cups on the table. "Sure. Thanks."

After filling their cups, she darted away.

Puzzled by her strange behavior, Rob mentally filed it away for later consideration, then turned back to Rebecca. "So you knew he was dead," he said, picking up the thread of their conversation. "What did you do then?"

"I called 9-1-1."

"From the bedroom?"

"No. The kitchen."

"Then what?"

"I went outside and waited for the police."

"Did you reenter the house at any point?"

She shook her head. "No. I...couldn't."

"What about your supplies? Surely you must have had something with you, some kind of equipment or tools, if you'd originally entered the house to tend his plants."

"Yes. I had my tote bag that I carry my supplies in. One of the policemen brought it out to me. The one who questioned me."

"What about the cat? Sadie, isn't it?"

"Yes. Sadie. I don't remember seeing her when I first entered the house. She must have been hiding somewhere. Under the sofa, perhaps. She does that sometimes. But when they brought Eric…the body out," she amended, wincing, "she slipped out the door. I caught her and held her to keep her from jumping into the ambulance with him."

He could see the tears building, the strain in her features, and wondered if this was all part of the act. In hopes of throwing her off balance, to trick her into slipping up, he changed the line of questioning. "You said you were fairly new in town."

She wrapped her hands around the coffee mug, as if needing the warmth to chase the chill from her body. "Yes. I moved here about six months ago."

"And immediately went into business for yourself."

"Yes."

He heard the pride in the single-worded response. "Had you ever owned a business before?"

She shook her head. "No. But I'd always dreamed of owning my own floral shop."

"So why move to Royal to open a business? Seems it would've made more sense to go into business in a town where you were known."

She fidgeted and he knew immediately that the question had made her uncomfortable.

"I was recently widowed," she explained slowly, as

if carefully choosing her words. "I wanted a fresh start. Someplace new, without…without any memories."

"I would think being surrounded by memories would be a comfort. Unless they were unpleasant ones," he added, watching her.

She stared at him, her face paling, her blue eyes filling with an anguish that had his gut clenching.

Tearing her gaze from his, she groped blindly for her purse. "I've told you all I know about Eric," she said as she slid from the booth. "If you'll excuse me, Mr. Cole, I really need to go."

Rob frowned as he listened to the officer's response to his query about the autopsy on Eric Chambers. "No prints?" he asked, frowning.

"None," the officer confirmed. "Whoever strangled him was careful. Probably wore surgical gloves of some type."

"Anything show up in his stomach? Any indication that he might have been drugged?"

"Only his dinner. Otherwise, he was clean."

Frustrated by the lack of any new leads on the case, Rob bit back a curse. "I appreciate the information. Let me know if y'all come up with anything new."

"I will. You do the same."

Rob hung up the phone and sank back in his chair, pushing his fingers through his hair.

No leads. No evidence. No suspects.

Other than Rebecca Todman.

Sighing, he sat up and reached for the mail he'd dropped on his desk. As he did, his gaze struck the fishbowl full of flowers that he'd bought at her shop. Frowning, he pushed aside the stack of mail and drew the bowl toward him. He stuck his nose in the flowers and inhaled deeply of the sweet floral scent, the lingering tartness of the citric fruits that filled the bowl's base.

His frown deepening, he leaned back and studied the arrangement. Classy. Fragrant. Feminine, yet not fussy. Fragile, yet with a hint of toughness.

Much like the woman who had designed it, he thought, unable to stop the stab of guilt that came along with the assessment.

Two days later and he still felt bad about his last interview with Rebecca Todman. He had questioned a lot of witnesses and suspects in his life, some more ruthlessly than others, but none had left him feeling more like a heel than had his last interview with her.

And well it should have, he concluded miserably. He'd tried his damnedest to catch her in a lie, to pry into her private life and prove that she was somehow responsible for Eric Chambers's murder. But nothing had panned out. Not motive. Not means. The only thing he could definitely nail her with was opportunity, which he could easily nail half the population of Royal with, as well.

Rebecca Todman hadn't killed Eric Chambers, he told himself. His search into her financial records had dissolved any lingering doubts about that. She had nothing to gain financially by murdering him. Though not a wealthy woman, she'd inherited enough money from her husband to make the down payment on her house in Royal and to set up her business, which appeared to be at least beginning to pay its own way.

No, Rebecca Todman wasn't the murderer, he thought ruefully, remembering the strained and haunted look on her face as he'd forced her to relive discovering Eric's body.

But there was still something about her that ate at

him. Some elusive something that kept him awake at night. But what? he asked himself, his frustration returning. Was it nothing more than physical attraction? A typical male response to the sight of a good-looking woman?

He leaned back in his chair and pulled at his chin as he gave that theory some thought. If so, he mused, then maybe it was time to get to know Rebecca Todman on another level. A level other than that of suspect.

A more intimate level.

With her knees and hands buried in the freshly turned soil of her cutting bed, Rebecca let the warmth of the late-afternoon sunshine and the heavenly scent of the flowers surrounding her work their special magic on her overwrought nerves. Calm. That's what she needed and what she sought each time she stepped out into her backyard oasis.

Though she loved her floral shop and felt a keen sense of pride each time she thought of the business she was building, it was only in her garden where she found true peace from the ugliness and brutality of her past. No old memories were allowed beyond the arch of the wisteria-draped garden gate. None were permitted to dig their way under the honeysuckle-covered picket fence, or pop up from the fertile soil like unwanted weeds. Only beautiful thoughts were allowed to bloom here, hopes and dreams that Rebecca had kept secreted away throughout the years of her marriage, protecting them from the destructive and cruel hand of her husband, Earl. Dreams of loving a man and being loved in return. Dreams of having children of her own someday.

She had planted those dreams right along with the climbing roses that now bloomed on the trellises at the rear of her property, nurtured them as carefully as she had the thick clusters of Shasta daisies that grew at the base of the birdbath that speared from the center of the cutting bed. And someday, just as the plants she tended had bloomed to life, she prayed so would her hopes and dreams for a normal life. A gentle and caring man to love, respect and protect her. Children to fill her home and her heart with their laughter and love.

But before she could have those things, Rebecca reminded herself, she had to first heal. Not physically. The bruises and marks Earl had left on her flesh had long since faded. It was the emotional scars that remained, leaving her crippled and incapable of even considering a relationship with another man.

She shook her head sadly, remembering her earlier foolishness in thinking that, with the move to Royal, she'd left behind all the ugliness of her past, healed herself completely from the lingering effects of Earl's abuse. She could remember in vivid detail the exact moment the revelation had occurred that had proved to her otherwise. At the time, she'd been at the New Hope Charity for battered women. Her purpose in making the visit had been an unselfish one. She'd wanted only to help other women who suffered similarly, offer them her support and encouragement.

Though she'd been a little nervous upon entering the shelter that first time, she'd approached the front desk, where she'd introduced herself to Andrea O'Rourke, a volunteer. They'd hit it off immediately and were chatting like old friends within minutes. Rebecca was filling out the forms Andrea had given her, required before becoming a volunteer, when the front door of the center had opened. Both had glanced up from the paperwork to find a female police officer ushering a sobbing woman inside.

One look at the woman's busted lip, the swelling that all but closed her left eye, her torn and blood-splattered clothing, and the trembling had started. Violent shudders had dragged the pen from Rebecca's fingers and drained the strength from her legs. She'd fainted dead away.

Oh, she'd been so smug, she thought now, upon reflection. So sure that she'd completely and successfully overcome all the effects of Earl's abuse. But she'd had pointed out to her, in a most vivid and humiliating way, that the physical scars might have faded, but the emotional ones were still very much with her.

But she would overcome them, too, she promised herself.

In the meantime, she would dream.

Sinking back on her heels, she let her gaze drift over the swaying, fragrant blooms that filled her garden, a brilliant testament to all the dreams she'd planted in this space. A man to love and cherish her. The children they would have, created from and nurtured by the mutual love and respect they had for each other.

She sighed as the scene blurred, the image of the man with whom she'd fall in love slowly building in her mind. He'd have to be strong, she told herself, and tipped back her head, closing her eyes while the picture of him grew, took shape. But never cruel. And handsome, she added, a soft smile curving her lips as the image began to sharpen and fill with detail. Tall, with thick, wavy hair. Deep blue eyes. Well-honed features. Broad shoulders. She could see him so clearly. So distinctly. So—

Her heart stumbled a beat and she flipped open her

eyes, realizing that the face she'd envisioned was none
other than the face of Rob Cole. Shaken, she struggled
to her feet. Rob Cole? she asked herself then pressed
her hands to her suddenly hot cheeks and shook her
head. No. Not him. The man terrified her. Infuriated her.

And had, from the moment he'd first appeared at her
shop, haunted her sleep and filled her dreams.

Irritated that she had so little control over her own
thoughts, she firmed her lips in a long-lost act of defi-
ance she struggled to recover each day. And what
woman wouldn't be fascinated by him? she asked herself with a sniff. He had the rugged good looks of an
outdoorsman and a muscular body that suggested that
whatever activities lured him there required a certain
level of strength and fitness.

But it wasn't his good looks or hard body that she
found herself thinking about, she admitted reluctantly.
It was his stone-faced expression, his gruff nature that
had her daydreaming of wrapping her arms around him
and teasing a smile from him.

Though he'd never shown her anything but the all-
business, investigative side of his personality, she was
sure there was another side to him, as well. A tender
and fun-loving side. It just needed nurturing, she told
herself. Love would draw out those qualities he kept
locked inside.

"And if you think you're the woman for the job,"
she muttered under her breath, "you've got another
think coming. Rob Cole is about as interested in devel-
oping a relationship with you as Sadie is."

Sadie, she remembered guiltily, and glanced around,
looking for her charge.

"Sadie," she called as she gathered her garden tools
and prepared to go inside. "Come on. It's time for our

dinner.'' She made her way through the cutting bed, careful to step on the stones she'd laid out and not on any of her plants. ''Sadie,'' she called again as she strode for the house.

When she reached the patio, she stooped to store her tools beneath the redwood potting table, then turned. Her shoulders drooped, when she saw that the cat hadn't appeared. Suspecting that Sadie had climbed the picket fence and gone home to Eric's house, just down the block, she crossed to the side gate and lifted the latch.

As she walked down the sidewalk, dread tightened her stomach with each step that brought her closer to Eric's house. She hadn't been to his home since the morning she'd found his body. She didn't even dare so much as glance in its direction as she drove past each day on her way to and from her shop. Couldn't. Not and keep the haunting images at bay.

Confronted with the strip of crime-scene tape still stretched across the drive, she curled her hands into determined fists, then made herself duck beneath it and hurried for the backyard.

''Sadie?'' she called uneasily. She tiptoed around to the patio, where she knew Sadie liked to sun. Spotting the cat curled up on the back stoop, waiting, Rebecca was sure, for Eric to come home and let her inside, she crossed to her. ''Oh, Sadie,'' she murmured sadly, as she stooped to scoop the cat up into her arms. ''Poor baby,'' she said sympathetically as she retraced her steps. ''You miss Eric, don't you, precious?''

''What are you doing here?''

Her heart leapt to her throat and she looked up to find Robert Cole standing in the middle of the drive, blocking her way.

''I...I came to get Sadie. She slipped away while I

was—'' She clamped her lips together, furious with herself for offering an explanation when she could just as easily ask the same thing of him. ''What are *you* doing here?'' she returned.

He slid his hands into his jean pockets and lifted a shoulder. ''Looking for you.'' He tipped his head in the direction of her house, where his sports car was parked at the curb. ''When I drove up, I saw you headed this way, so I parked my car and followed.''

Sure that he'd come to question her again, she drew the cat to her chest, as if the animal were a shield. ''As I've told you repeatedly, there's nothing more I can tell you about Eric's murder.''

''I didn't come to question you about the case.''

If possible, she found that revelation even more unnerving than if he'd stated that he was there to arrest her. ''Then what do you want?''

He scrunched his mouth to one side and looked away, as if he found his explanation distasteful. ''To apologize.''

''For what?''

He scuffed his boot across the loose rock on the drive, then glanced over at her. The effect on her system was the same as if she'd stuck her finger into an electrical socket. The blue in his eyes was softer now, more open, giving her a glimpse at that hidden quality she was so sure was there inside.

''For being so tough on you the other day. You were upset when you left the diner, and I wanted you to know that I was sorry about that.''

Reminded of his callous treatment, she lifted her chin. ''Yes, I was upset. And understandably so. Finding Eric was upsetting enough, but to be forced by you to relive the incident was sheer torture.''

He turned and gestured for her to walk with him. "As I said, I'm sorry. But the questions were necessary, in order for me to establish your innocence."

She jerked to a stop and looked up at him, eyes wide. "You thought *I* killed Eric?"

He lifted the crime-scene tape. When she didn't make a move to slip under it, he placed a hand on the small of her back and urged her beneath it. "Yes, you were a suspect." He ducked beneath the tape, then dropped it and slid his hands into his pockets again. Inclining his head, he indicated for her to walk with him.

She did so, hugging Sadie against her breasts. "A suspect," she repeated, stunned that he'd think she had killed Eric. She looked over at him. "But why me?"

"Opportunity. You had a key to his house and the perfect alibi." He arched a brow at her questioning look. "Home alone," he said, reminding her of the alibi she'd given to the police. "Impossible to prove or disprove."

They reached the edge of her drive. "But it's the truth," she insisted, turning to face him. "I *was* home alone."

He reached out and took the cat from her, his expression closed again, not offering a clue as to whether he believed her or not. "Hard to prove, either way." He cradled the animal along his arm and chest and stroked her head. "Sure wish you could talk," he said to the cat. "I'll bet you could tell us who murdered Eric."

Rebecca hugged her arms around her middle to hide a shiver. "It's difficult to believe a murder was committed in Royal." She shivered again and glanced uneasily down the street. "And in this neighborhood, no less."

He glanced her way, his stroking drawing a deep, satisfied purr from the cat. "You keep your doors locked, don't you?"

"Yes. Windows, too." The blood slowly drained from her face as she stared at him. "You don't think that whoever killed Eric would return and kill again, do you?"

He lifted a shoulder and passed the cat back to her. "Who knows? We still don't know who murdered Eric or why."

She buried her cheek against the cat's fur. "If you're trying to frighten me," she said shakily, "you're certainly doing a good job."

"I'm not trying to frighten you. Just making sure you're taking the necessary precautions." He slid his hands into his pockets again. "But that's not why I stopped by. I was wondering if you'd go out to dinner with me tomorrow night."

The invitation caught Rebecca totally off guard. "Dinner?" she repeated. "Tomorrow night?" At his nod, she could only stare. For a moment she allowed herself to believe that he found her attractive, interesting, that he wanted to get to know her better. Maybe even develop a relationship. She even let herself go so far as to believe she could go out with him without suffering a panic attack. That she could talk and laugh and tease, just like any other woman, without her stomach knotting up or her hands growing damp.

Then she remembered him initially saying he'd dropped by to apologize, and all the air whooshed from her inflated dreams, as she realized that his dinner invitation was offered for no other reason than to make amends, just as his invitation to take her for coffee had been.

"No," she murmured, and turned away to hide her disappointment. "I'm sorry. I already have plans."

Three

Rob had received rejections before, had accepted them
and gone on down the road, without giving the woman
who'd turned him down another thought. But he found
he couldn't accept Rebecca's refusal to have dinner
with him…and it wasn't his ego standing in the way,
either. It was *her.* That mysterious something about her
that haunted him and had almost from the moment he'd
laid eyes on her. He went to bed thinking about her,
woke up thinking about her. Even during the day while
he was working on the murder case, she was on his
mind.

Yet it wasn't the investigation that kept her foremost
in his thoughts. At least, not since he'd convinced himself of her innocence. It was something else. Something
transient. Elusive. Some niggling something that danced
just out of his reach, no matter how hard he grasped at
it.

A man who enjoyed complex riddles and puzzles, one who liked nothing better than chipping away at a problem until he'd reached the core of the matter, Rob tackled his fixation with Rebecca Todman in the same methodical way in which he worked on a case. He reviewed every note he'd taken of their interviews. Analyzed from every possible angle the profile he'd built of her life prior to her move to Royal. Stared for hours at her picture, both the one taken at the crime scene and the one he'd found of her on the Internet buried in the Dallas newspaper's archives, hoping to discover what it was about her that bugged him.

But it was when he least expected it that he found his answer.

He'd been asleep at the time, locked in the bony-fingered clutches of the nightmare he'd carried with him from boyhood into adulthood. Sweat had covered his body and soaked his sheets…yet an icy fear had banded his chest and chilled his skin.

The dream was always the same, varying only slightly from time to time. In the dream he was running from his father, his arms pumping and his lungs burning with the effort to escape the beating he knew he'd receive if his father caught him. But as hard as he ran, his father was always right behind him, his arms outstretched, his hands only inches from grabbing Rob by the scruff of the neck.

On this particular night, one of the variations of the dream slipped into play. While running, Rob tripped and fell, slamming face first onto the hard ground. He quickly rolled, an instinctive movement he'd learned over the years, one that had saved him from more than one beating. But this time his father had anticipated the move and was already grabbing for him. Sobbing, Rob threw an arm over his head to block the blows he knew were coming and dug his heels into the ground, trying to scramble away.

It was at that point that he'd woken up.

It had taken a moment for his breathing to slow. Another second or two for the chill to leave his skin.

And that's when the similarities had hit him.

The arm thrown over the head. The frightened, cowering position. That's what it was about Rebecca that had haunted him, he realized. That's why she always seemed so uneasy around him. So nervous. The afternoon he'd caught her unawares in her greenhouse she had reacted to Rob's touch in the same manner he always had when his father had come after him.

Someone had abused Rebecca. More than likely a man, judging by her reaction to Rob. Her father? he asked himself as he drove to her shop. An old boyfriend? Her deceased husband? The identity of the abuser, at this point, was moot. What was important to Rob was to prove to Rebecca Todman that he wasn't a violent man, that she had nothing to fear from him.

The thought of her being afraid of him or of her thinking that he'd ever cause her—or anyone, for that matter—bodily harm was something he wouldn't tolerate. He'd lived with abuse throughout his childhood and had despised his father for the cruelties he'd subjected Rob to. To even suspect that Rebecca had suffered similarly made Rob cold and queasy. But to imagine that she thought *he,* Rob Cole, would physically hurt her, that she might feel even a fraction of the fear and hate that he had felt toward his father…

Well, she wouldn't, he promised himself. He'd see to that.

Unsure what he planned to say or do to convince her

that he was nothing like the person who had abused her, he parked his car at the curb and entered her shop. The bell chimed musically overhead, announcing his entrance. Business was brisk, with several customers already lined up at the counter. Rebecca stood behind it, smiling as she offered care instructions to a customer as she rang up a sale. At the sound of the chime she glanced up, her smile fading when her gaze met his.

He nodded politely, then turned down an aisle to browse, wanting the shop to clear before he approached her. He waited until she was walking the last customer to the door, then moved into the center aisle behind her, blocking her return to the counter. When she turned and found him standing there, her face paled and she clasped her hands at her waist and nervously began to twist them.

"I'm not here to discuss Eric's case," he said, hoping, if that was the cause for her unease, to put her mind at rest. He glanced around, trying to think of a reason to offer for the visit—one she wouldn't find threatening. "A friend of mine's mother is in the hospital," he said, spotting a balloon with "Get Well" emblazoned on a rainbow across its center. "I'd like to take her something."

Swallowing hard, Rebecca smoothed her hands across the front of her apron as she eased around him and made her way back to the counter. "Cut flowers or a potted plant?"

Rob followed. "I'll leave that up to you."

She stepped quickly behind the counter, as if she needed that protective barrier between them. "Roses are always nice, but a common choice and will only last a few days. I'd suggest a blooming plant." She reached behind her to select a pot of colorful begonias from her worktable. "Something she can enjoy while in the hospital and after she returns home, as well."

"Whatever you think best."

He pulled out his wallet and dropped his credit card on the counter, watching as she wrapped the pot in pink foil and tied a ribbon and fancy bow around it. "I'd still like to take you out to dinner," he said quietly, watching for her reaction.

Her fingers fumbled on the bow. She drew in a long breath, then forced herself to finish securing it. "My business is new," she hedged, avoiding his gaze, "and takes up quite a bit of my time." She gestured toward a rack on the counter. "If you'd like to select a card, I'll attach it to the plant for you."

Rob plucked one out and quickly signed his name. "You have to eat," he reminded her.

"Yes, but—" The phone rang, saving her from responding. With a murmured "excuse me," she lifted the portable from the base and tucked it between shoulder and ear as she rang up the sale.

"In Bloom," she said into the receiver. "Yes, Mrs. Carter," she said as she swiped Rob's credit card through the machine, then slid it back across the counter to him, "we're still on for five-thirty. I'll be bringing along several plants for your approval, which I think will do well in your home."

Rob signed the credit card slip Rebecca placed on the counter, listening to the conversation as he returned the card and receipt to his wallet.

"I'll be there promptly at five-thirty," Rebecca assured the woman. "See you then." She hung up the phone, then pushed the potted plant across the counter and forced a smile. "I hope your friend's mother enjoys the plant, Mr. Cole."

"Rob," he corrected.

She averted her gaze, her cheeks turning as bright a pink as the begonias. "All right…Rob."

When he didn't make a move to leave, she busied herself tidying the counter, continuing to avoid his gaze. "Is there something else I can help you with?"

He looked around, the phone conversation he'd overhead having offered him the perfect opening he needed to see Rebecca again. "Yeah. As a matter of fact, there is. I need some plants for my house."

A frown knitted her brow. "What type of plants?"

"I don't know. Just plants."

"Before I can recommend something, I'd need to know what type of lighting you have in your home and what size plants it can accommodate, plus the style of your decor."

Pleased that he'd succeeded in boxing her into a corner she couldn't wriggle out of, he lifted a shoulder. "I don't have a clue about that kind of stuff. Guess we'll need to book an appointment for you to come out and take a look at my place. How about tomorrow evening at six?"

Only minutes after Rob left, the bell chimed again over the entrance to Rebecca's shop. Fearing it was Rob returning, she glanced toward the door to find it was Andrea O'Rourke breezing into her shop.

"Andrea," she said in relief as she rounded the counter to greet her friend. "Am I ever glad to see you."

Andrea raised an eyebrow. "If I'd known you were that desperate for customers, I'd have dropped by earlier."

Rebecca laughed weakly. "I'm not desperate for customers, just a friendly face."

Immediately concerned, Andrea looped her arm through Rebecca's. "Bad day?"

"No," Rebecca replied, grateful once again that she had gathered the courage to visit the New Hope Charity for battered women. Even though she'd never found the courage to return as a volunteer, she had gained a friend from the experience. Her friendship with Andrea had grown until Rebecca had found the courage to share with Andrea the horrors of her abusive past. Over the months since, she had sought Andrea's guidance and advice several times. "Just an unsettling customer."

Andrea studied her as they walked to the counter. "Want to talk about it?"

Rebecca pulled out stools for the two to sit on. "It's silly, really," she said, embarrassed to admit to her fear of Rob.

"It isn't, if it upsets you," Andrea assured her. "Now, tell me what's happened."

Rebecca drew in a long breath, then released it on a rush of air. "It's Rob Cole."

Andrea nodded, already aware of Rob having questioned Rebecca several times. "Has he been hassling you again about the Chambers murder case?"

Rebecca shook her head. "No...not exactly."

"What, then?"

"He was in the shop earlier and made an appointment for me to come out and evaluate his home for interior plants."

Andrea looked at her curiously. "But that's a good thing, isn't it? More business for your shop?"

Rebecca dropped her gaze to stare at the fingers she'd

laced on her lap. "Yes. It definitely means more business."

"Uh-oh," Andrea muttered dryly. "I hear a 'but' coming."

"It's just that—" Rebecca began, then stopped and caught her lower lip between her teeth.

"That what?" Andrea pressed.

Rebecca shot from the stool. "He scares me, okay?" she said, pacing away in frustration. "Every time I see him my stomach ties itself in knots and my hands get all clammy."

"Do other men affect you similarly?"

Rebecca stopped for a moment, considering, then slowly turned and retraced her steps. "No. Not really. At least, not in the same way."

"Do you suppose your reaction to Rob is different because you might be attracted to him?"

Rebecca gulped, but couldn't bring herself to admit that Andrea might be right.

Smiling softly in understanding, Andrea reached to catch Rebecca's hand in hers. "I'd say you've taken another big step on the road to recovery."

Rebecca rolled her eyes. "If that's true, then why do I panic every time I'm around him?"

"You know the answer to that as well as I do. But Rob isn't going to hurt you, Rebecca," Andrea reminded her gently. "I know he's gruff and looks mean enough to spit nails, but he really is a nice man underneath."

"I'm sure he is," Rebecca agreed readily. "It's just that—"

"You think all men are like your husband," Andrea finished for her. She squeezed Rebecca's hand, then released it with a sigh. "They're not. I know it doesn't do any good to tell you that, but it's true. There are a lot of really kind and loving men out there. Unfortunately, your husband was one of the exceptions.''

Rebecca shook her head. ''I know you're right. At least, intellectually I do. But here,'' she said, clutching a hand to her stomach, ''is a totally different story. The appointment isn't until tomorrow afternoon, and already my stomach feels as if an entire troop of Boy Scouts are inside practicing their knot-tying skills.''

Laughing, Andrea rose. ''You'll do fine,'' she said, and draped a companionable arm along Rebecca's shoulders. ''If it'll help, just tell yourself that this is a business call, not a social one, and you'll send those Boy Scouts packing.''

''It's a business call, not a social one,'' Rebecca reminded herself, drawing upon Andrea's advice as she drove down the narrow two-lane road, following the directions Rob had given her. Though she'd been tempted to call him several times during the day to cancel their appointment, she couldn't afford to let a business opportunity like this pass her by. Not when the client was a longtime and well-respected citizen of Royal with the power to make or break her business, if he chose to do so.

She spotted the entrance to his ranch, marked by the large stone columns and the iron arch with the Circle ''C'' forged across its width. Surprised by the simplicity of the entrance, she craned her neck to peer back at it in the rearview mirror as she drove over the cattle guard.

Oleanders, she thought. Watermelon-pink oleanders planted in front of the stone walls that curved in a downward slope from each side of the gate would be the perfect backdrop, creating a more colorful and dramatic entrance to his ranch. And lantana, she thought further, the design building in her mind. A bright golden variety placed in front of the oleanders would offer the perfect contrast in both height and hue.

But as she turned her gaze to the drive again, thoughts of oleanders and lantana flew from her mind as she spotted the contemporary log home in the distance, nestled among a grove of trees. High banks of windows peeked from between the highest branches of the trees, while a stone chimney rose like a beacon from the roof's center. She slowly pulled to a stop in front of the house, unable to take her eyes off the impressive structure. She wasn't sure what she'd expected Rob Cole's home to look like, but she was certain her perceptions hadn't included anything like this! His home was absolutely gorgeous and strategically placed on the land to take advantage of all the panoramic views the natural landscape offered.

Anxious to see if the interior equaled the exterior's care in design, she quickly gathered her tote bag and hopped down from her van. As she hurried along the stone path that led to the front porch, her mind raced ahead with ideas. White alyssum, coreopsis and lavender to border the stone pathway. Oversize redwood pots with tall topiaries of ivy placed at either side of the entrance. A low planting of verbena or perhaps rose moss cascading over the sides of the planters and to the porch floor below. An intimate grouping of bent willow chairs on the wide front porch and a swing suspended from the ceiling where the porch wrapped the side of the house would create the perfect spot to entertain guests or wile away a lazy afternoon.

She was so engrossed with her plans that she forgot

to knock. She jumped, startled, when the door opened and Rob stepped out. If anything, he seemed more intimidating than ever.

And more handsome.

Instead of the slacks and sports coat he'd worn each time he questioned her, he was dressed more casually in jeans and a faded chambray shirt, the blue in the shirt shades lighter than that in his eyes.

"Have any trouble finding the place?"

As usual, his expression was stony, his question clipped, his voice gruff. Her nervousness returned with a vengeance. "N-no," she stammered, taking an unconscious step back. "Your directions were easy to follow."

"Good." He moved to the side. "Come inside and take a look around."

She tightened her fingers on her tote bag's strap. *A business appointment,* she reminded herself, and made herself move past him. Once inside, she paused and stole a quick glance around while she waited for him to deal with the door. Her gaze was immediately drawn upward by shards of colorful light dancing on the log walls, and to a stained glass skylight at the peak of the twenty-foot-high entry hall.

Her nervousness melted away as she stared in awe at the gorgeous panels of stained glass, each depicting a continuing scene of low hills and vast sky, much like the view she'd noticed behind the house as she'd driven up.

"How lovely," she murmured.

Rob looked up as he closed the door, following her gaze. "I like it. Had it made by a local craftsman when the house was built two years ago. Haven't done much with the place since, though."

She dropped her gaze, her mouth agape in amazement. "Two years? And you haven't done anything to your home? Why not?"

He lifted a shoulder. "Just wasn't a priority, I guess." He gestured for her to precede him into the large room that opened off the entry.

One step into the room and Rebecca was hurrying to the far wall of windows, a frame of sorts for the span of green pastures and blue sky beyond. Horses of all different sizes and breeds grazed beneath a late-afternoon sun. "East?" she asked, glancing over her shoulder for confirmation of the exposure.

"Yeah. I've considered covering the windows. That morning sun can be a bitch."

Her eyes shot wide. "Cover them? And lose this view?" She quickly made note of the placement of furniture in the room as she sought a solution. "You might consider shutters. They would allow you to control the amount of light without sacrificing the view."

With something to focus on now besides her nervousness, she dug in her tote and pulled out a tape. "Here," she said, and thrust one end to him. "Hold this." She crossed to the opposite end of the windows, stretching out the tape, while Rob held his end steady.

She pulled a pad from her tote bag and made a few notations, then rewound the tape. "Plantation shutters would cost a fortune, but worth every penny. If you had them stained to match the logs, they'd blend so well you'd hardly notice them. I can give you the name of a decorator, if you like." She turned slowly, letting her gaze rise to the heavy beams overhead. "This ceiling height is tall enough to accommodate a ten- maybe even a twelve-foot Norfolk pine without any problem," she said thoughtfully. "Perfect for that corner over there," she said, pointing, then sucked in a breath when she caught a glimpse of the atrium that speared off the den and out onto the patio.

She hurried toward the space. "This would be the perfect spot for a rock garden! You could berm up some areas with soil," she said, moving a hand through the air as if drawing in the varying elevations, "creating height and dimension. Stack some decorative boulders about. Plant different varieties of fern and ground covers in the nooks between. Maybe even add a water feature. There's definitely room. A fountain," she said, then cried, "No!" all but breathless now with excitement. "A koi pond! With water lilies, arrowhead and canna—"

Rob watched her, amazed by the startling transformation from scared-of-her-shadow woman to this incredibly vibrant and animated woman. He shook his head. "Do you always get this excited about a new project?"

She whirled, as if she'd totally forgotten his presence. Color shot to her cheeks. "I—I'm sorry," she stammered. "It was merely a suggestion."

Rob shrugged as he crossed to join her. "No problem. I've just never seen anyone get so pumped up over a few plants."

"Oh, it isn't just the plants," she told him quickly, then turned to look around her, unable to hide her fascination with his home. "It's this house. There are so many wonderful possibilities. So much natural light. So many views. I can't believe you haven't taken advantage of it all before now."

Rob glanced around, trying to see his home through her eyes. Though he had designed the house himself, he'd never really had an interest in decorating it. A house, to him, was just a place to sleep, a place to work.

And he certainly wouldn't be considering cluttering the place up with a bunch of plants now, if it wasn't the only way he could think of to see Rebecca Todman again.

"That's why you're here," he reminded her, then led her into the kitchen.

An hour later, Rebecca returned to the kitchen, after being taken on a tour of the entire house by Rob, her mind still reeling from all she'd seen. If he allowed her to place plants in all the areas she'd made note of, it would cost him a small fortune, she knew.

Reminded of that, she said, "We haven't discussed a budget yet."

He frowned. "Budget?"

"How much money you want to spend on the project," she explained.

He shrugged. "Whatever it takes, I guess."

Which really wasn't an answer at all, Rebecca thought in frustration. "What if I draw you up a quote that includes all the possibilities, then you can look it over and let me know what, if anything, you'd like done?"

"Fair enough."

With the appointment at an end, Rebecca slipped the straps of her tote bag over her shoulder, preparing to leave. "I should be able to have the quote ready by tomorrow afternoon." She forced herself to offer her hand to him, the same as she would to any potential client at the conclusion of an appointment. "Thank you for your time. It's been a true pleasure seeing your home."

He frowned as he took her hand in his. "You're leaving?"

"Well, yes," she said in surprise. "I've got all the information I need for now."

"Can I offer you a drink first?"

Rebecca gulped when he didn't release her hand, her stomach knotting as panic began to set in. "Thank you, but no. I really do need to go." She tried to pull away again, but he tightened his grip. The panic twisted tighter and her breathing became more rapid.

Rob saw the fear flash in her eyes, felt the tremble of it in her fingers. "Are you afraid of me?"

"No," she said too quickly, then swallowed and gave her hand another pull. "Please, Mr. Cole, I really need to go."

"Rob," he reminded her, but released her hand. "When you deliver the quote tomorrow, do you think you could cut two hours out of your schedule?"

"I suppose I could," she replied uneasily. "Though I'm sure it won't take that long for me to go over the bid with you."

"Probably not." He gestured for her to precede him to the front door. "But it'll take us that long to eat dinner."

Rebecca propped herself up in bed and settled the sketch pad over her lap. Inhaling deeply, she flipped open the cover, then sank back against the pillows when confronted with the blank page, all the old inadequacies returning to haunt her.

Could she sketch the design she'd promised? she asked herself as the panic edged closer. It had been so long since she'd attempted to sketch anything, much less something for someone else to see. Another pleasure Earl had robbed her of with his demeaning comments about her artistic abilities and the time she wasted on a hobby he claimed she had so little talent for.

"Earl's not here any longer," she reminded herself sternly, and forced herself to pluck a pencil from the box she'd placed on the bed at her side. Rolling it between her fingers, she stared at the intimidating blank page. Then, firming her lips, she made the first sweeping arc, setting the boundary for earth and sky. She made another stroke. Another. And soon her hand was fairly flying over the page as she roughed in the shape of Rob's house and the trees that surrounded it, pulling from her memory the details she'd unconsciously stored there during her visit.

The alarm clock on her bedside table clicked away the minutes and hours as she tossed aside one colored pencil, only to snatch up another, her absorption in the project complete. The log walls of his home grew as she shaded them in, gaining texture and depth, as did the complicated angles of the roof. She sketched in the winding walkway that led to the front door, then added the lavender, coreopsis and white alyssum that she'd envisioned bordering it.

With her tongue caught between her teeth, she attacked the front porch, quickly sketching in the cedar pots with their ivy-draped topiaries, the bent willow furniture and the swing.

When she finished, she fell back against the pillows, exhausted, but pleased with her design.

The clock on the bedside table read 3:47 a.m.

Tired, but hyped with nervous anticipation, the next afternoon Rebecca drove to her appointment with Rob. She had dressed as she would for any appointment, refusing to place any more importance on this one than she would on one with any other potential client. So what if he had invited her to stay for dinner after they reviewed the bid? It was a casual invitation, a natural conclusion to any business meeting held in the evening. People did it all the time.

But if that was the case, then why did she currently feel as if she were driving herself to her own execution?

She parked her van in front of his house and sat there for a moment, staring at the front door while she tried to work up the courage to leave the safety of her vehicle. Before she could, the van door opened at her side, making her jump.

Rob stepped into the opening. "Sorry. Didn't mean to startle you. I was in the barn when you drove up. Thought you might need some help carrying stuff in."

Rebecca fumbled for her tote on the passenger seat. "No. I only have this."

He stepped back, giving her room to climb down. "I thought you'd be bringing plants for me to look at?"

She eased around him. "Not this trip. But I did bring some horticulture books, in case you weren't familiar with some of the plants I've suggested."

Rob cupped a hand at her elbow and guided her toward the front door. He felt her stiffen at the contact, and knew that he wasn't any closer than he had been the day before to proving to her that she had nothing to fear from him. Clamping down on his frustration, he released her arm to open the front door. "If it's all right with you, I thought we'd talk out on the patio."

Rebecca avoided his gaze, nodded and followed him through the house. When they reached the patio, he pulled out a chair for her at a wrought-iron table, then, after seating her, moved to a grill positioned at the edge of the patio. He lifted the lid, and smoke billowed in a cloud around his head.

"Coals won't be hot enough for a few minutes yet," he said, replacing the lid. "We can look over your bid while we're waiting."

Rebecca wiped her damp palms down her thighs. "Okay." She opened her tote and pulled out the quote, as well as the sketches she'd made and a couple of the horticulture books she'd brought along. As Rob seated himself in the chair next to hers, she spread the sketches out over the table. "We didn't discuss exterior plantings," she began, forcing herself to focus on the designs she'd created and not on the nearness of the man at her side, "but I took the liberty of making a few sketches for your consideration."

Rob picked up the first drawing and lifted a brow as he studied it, noting not only the naturalness of the landscape design she'd created, but the skill and accuracy with which she'd captured his home. He cast an appraising glance her way. "You did these?"

"Yes," she said, and laced her fingers to keep from snatching the drawing back.

His only response was a grunt.

Rob flipped to the next sketch, this one an interior drawing of the atrium she'd gotten so carried away with the day before. He drew his brows together as he studied it, amazed at the amount of detail she'd incorporated into the design. The concept was just as she'd described, only better now that it was embellished with the colorful plantings and boulders she'd drawn in.

Rebecca watched his face, her hopes sagging, convinced by his silence, his frown, that he didn't care for her proposal. She reached for the drawing. "If you don't like it, I can come up with something else."

Rob held the sketch up out of her reach. "Who said I didn't like it?"

She drew her hands back to clasp in her lap again. "It was your expression. You were frowning," she explained when he looked at her in puzzlement.

He grunted again, a sound that indicated neither acceptance nor disgust, then pointed to a plant. "What are these?"

"*Dryopteris marginalis.* Wood fern," she clarified, giving the more common name. "And these are a variety of hosta," she said, indicating a cluster of wide-leafed plants with tall, slender spikes topped with delicate lavender blooms. "They require little direct sunlight and would adapt well to an interior garden."

He gathered up the sketches and the bid and handed them back to her, then pushed back from his chair and headed for the grill.

Rebecca's heart sank, sure that she'd lost the job. She slipped the bid and sketches back into her tote, trying her best to hide her disappointment.

"How long will it take?"

Rebecca glanced up to stare at the back of his head in confusion. "Excuse me?"

He looked over his shoulder. "To get the job done. How long will it take?"

"Well…I'm not sure," she replied, her mind reeling. "It will depend on how much of my design you want to incorporate."

He waved a hand at the tote where she'd placed the sketches. "All of it. How long?" he repeated, and turned to lift the grill lid.

She stared, watching as he dropped two steaks over the hot coals, unable to believe that he was giving her the job without so much as a glance at the bid itself. "I can have the interior plants in place within a couple of days,'' she said slowly, trying not to think of what a job this size would add, not only to her checkbook but to her reputation, as well. ''The atrium will take a bit longer, as I'll have to make arrangements to have the koi pond built.''

''What about the exterior stuff? Do you do that work yourself or subcontract it out?''

''I'd rather do the work myself, although I can subcontract the job to a professional landscaper, if you prefer.''

Rob closed the lid, slicing off the smoke that rose from the sizzling steaks. ''When would you have the time?'' He turned, dragging his hands across the seat of his jeans. ''I mean, with your hours at the shop and all.''

''Evenings and Sundays. Unless you're in a hurry,'' she told him quickly. ''If you are, then I would need to arrange for someone else to do the work.''

Realizing that he'd just been handed on a silver platter another opportunity to spend more time with Rebecca, Rob shrugged. ''I'm in no hurry. In fact, I wouldn't mind getting my hands a little dirty myself. If you could use the help, that is,'' he added, then tipped his head toward the grill before she could respond. ''We've got a few minutes before the steaks are done.'' He held out a hand. ''Let's take a walk and you can give me a rundown on what all you've got in mind for the place.''

Four

Rebecca caught herself just shy of shrinking away from the offered hand. The wide palm, the slightly curled, blunt-tipped fingers. A masculine hand. A strong hand. A hand capable of jerking her to her feet and shoving her up hard against a wall or slapping her senseless. To Earl the process itself had never mattered. It was the result that was important.

Submission. Pain.

And his hands were usually his weapon of choice.

She drew in a shuddery breath. He's not Earl, she told herself as she forced the ugly memories to a far corner of her mind. He's a client. And the hand extended toward her was nothing but a gentlemanly gesture.

Though it was difficult, she made herself place her hand in his and allowed him to help her to her feet. But as soon as she was standing, she pulled away.

But his grip on her tightened, refusing to let her go. Not with enough strength to hurt her. Not as Earl had always done. But with just enough firmness to let her know that he wasn't letting go.

"I didn't see any sketches of the backyard," he said, and led her toward the edge of the stone patio, as if unaware of her discomfort.

"I—I didn't make any." She cleared her throat, praying he didn't hear the tremble in her voice or feel the dampness slicking her palm. She tried not to think about the power in the fingers curled around hers or the intimacy of their joined hands, but forced herself to focus instead on the plans she'd made for his home. "It seemed a shame to alter it, when nature has already provided you with the perfect landscape."

"You'd know best." He stopped and turned to face the rear of his home. "And the patio?" he asked, drawing her around to stand beside him. "What do you have in mind for it?"

It was hard to concentrate on his question, what with the heat of his body radiating between their palms, the tart, male scent of his aftershave filling her senses with each breath she drew.

The job, she lectured herself sternly. *Focus on the job*.

"Nothing too fussy," she said, succeeding for the moment to hold the panic at bay. "A few potted plants scattered about. Another water feature. A standing fountain is what I had in mind. But if you'd prefer, I could have the contractor who'll build the koi pond construct another smaller pond out of stone. Perhaps one with a waterfall tumbling over a tower of stacked rocks."

He narrowed his eyes at the patio, as if trying to

visualize what she'd described. "I like that," he said, and gave his head a decisive nod. "What else?"

She tugged her hand from his to point...and this time, to her relief, he allowed her to break the contact. "I thought I'd place a birdbath there at the edge of the patio where the atrium juts out from the house. And hang feeders from that large oak that shades the breakfast-room windows. It would give you a perfect view of the birds' activities from your breakfast-room table, plus the birds will help with any insect problems that might arise. The plants would also attract..."

Rob eased back a little so that he could watch her as she talked on, describing the types of feeders she planned to hang and the birds and butterflies they would attract, noting the flush on her cheeks and the animation that lit her eyes as her enthusiasm grew. He didn't bother to tell her that he seldom sat at his breakfast-room table, consuming most of his meals on a stool at the bar, and would, more than likely, never enjoy the bird sanctuary she planned to create for him.

As he watched her, the wind kicked up, tugging her hair from where she'd tucked it behind her ear, and whipped it across her cheek. Without thinking, he reached out to push the strands back, not wanting his view of her profile interrupted. She ducked at the action, as if dodging a blow.

That hole opened in Rob's stomach again, spilling that same gut-churning acid into his stomach. Setting his face in grim lines, he silently cursed the man who had instilled this level of fear in her.

"Sorry," he said, and drew back his hand to shove it into his pocket. "I only wanted to straighten your hair."

Dropping her chin, she threaded the wayward strands

behind her ear, her cheeks blazing. "That's okay. I…you just startled me."

Which was only partly the truth, he knew. But he wanted *all* the truth. He wanted her to open up to him, to tell him about the abuse and the man who had abused her. More, he wanted her to trust him, to believe him when he told her he meant her no harm. "Are you always this jumpy? Or is it just when you're around me?"

"Yes—no."

"Well, which is it?"

Rebecca pushed her hands into fists at her sides, furious with him for not letting the embarrassing incident pass and with herself for overreacting. "No, I'm not always this jumpy. And yes, you do seem to have an adverse effect on my nervous system."

"Why?"

When she pressed her lips together and remained silent, her gaze fixed on the rear of his home, Rob moved in front of her. He crooked a finger beneath her chin and forced her gaze to his. "Why?" he repeated quietly.

Rebecca felt tears burning the back of her throat and gulped them back. "Because you do frighten me. I know you don't mean to," she hastened to add when his brows came together in question, "but you do."

"Why?"

She groaned and turned away, raking her fingers through her hair and holding it back from her face.

"Rebecca…"

At his persistence, she whirled. "Because you're a man, that's why! You're bigger than me and stronger than me and you could hurt me if you wanted to." As soon as the words were out, she clapped her hands over her mouth, appalled by what she'd said, by what she'd almost revealed.

He took a step toward her and caught her hands. He held his gaze steady on hers as he slowly drew them down. "Have I ever done anything that would make you think that I meant to harm you?"

The quietness in his voice, the hurt in it, left her feeling weak and utterly foolish. "No," she murmured, and dropped her gaze.

"And I wouldn't hurt you. You have my word on that. Rebecca. Look at me."

Though she would have preferred to crawl into a hole and never have to look him in the face again, she forced her head up.

He gave her hands a reassuring squeeze. "That's better."

Her breath caught in her throat.

"What?"

"You…you smiled."

"So?"

"You've never done that before."

He quirked a brow. "Really?"

"Yes. Really."

"Tell you what," he said, and gave her hands another squeeze. "If you promise not to jump every time I get within arm's reach of you, I'll promise to smile more often. How's that for a deal?"

Though Rebecca wasn't at all sure she could uphold her end of the bargain, she was willing to try…if only for the chance to see that bone-melting smile of his again.

"It's a deal."

Rebecca all but raced from her van to her shop and back again as she loaded the potted plants and garden accessories she'd chosen for Rob's house and yard.

Though she kept telling herself her excitement was due to the new project she was about to begin, she knew that was only part of the cause.

The truth was, she couldn't wait to see Rob. Though she'd never fully relaxed the evening before while they were eating the dinner he'd prepared, she had managed to enjoy herself a little. And him. He'd helped by keeping his end of the bargain and smiling a little, even teasing a few from her.

As she made the drive to his ranch, her excitement built until she was sure she would explode if she didn't arrive soon. Once there, she didn't hesitate, as she'd done before, but hopped from her van and headed straight for the front door. She knocked, then smoothed her palms down her khaki slacks while she waited for him to answer. When he didn't, she leaned to peek through one of the glass panels that framed either side of the massive door. Finding the house dark and no sign of movement within, she swallowed back her disappointment and turned back to the van.

Before calling it a day, on a hunch, Rob dropped by the police station and requested permission to examine Eric Chambers's home computer, hoping to find a clue on the system to who might have wanted Eric dead.

"Sorry," the detective in charge of the case told him. "We've sent the computer to Dallas for analysis."

"Dallas?" Rob repeated.

The detective lifted a shoulder. "Closest lab with a computer specialist on staff."

Frustrated, Rob pushed a hand through his hair. "When will you get it back?"

"We asked for a rush job, but I figure it'll be at least a week, maybe two. The techs are backed up," the detective explained, "what with all the computer crimes currently on the books."

Scowling, Rob turned for the door. "Give me a call when you get it back, okay?"

"Sure thing," the detective called after him.

Discouraged by the obstacles that kept popping up, blocking his progress on the investigation, Rob climbed into his sports car. He sat there for a moment, drumming his fingers on the steering wheel, before it occurred to him that Eric probably had use of another computer, this one at Wescott Oil. Knowing that Seb was the only man with the authority to release the computer, he started the car's engine and pulled away from the curb, headed for the corporate offices of Wescott Oil.

But when he arrived, Seb had already left for the day. It took Rob over an hour to track him down. He finally found him seated at the bar in the Texas Cattleman's Club, nursing a beer.

Scowling, Rob slid onto the bar stool next to him. "You're a hell of a man to bring to ground. Even your secretary didn't know where to find you."

With a calm that had Rob's bad mood scaling upward another degree, Seb sipped at his beer. "Exactly. What she doesn't know, she can't repeat." He held his beer up before his face and studied the amber liquid, then cut a glance at Rob. "Last I heard, it wasn't a crime for a man to skip out early from work. Especially if he was the boss."

Rob lifted a hand, signaling the bartender to bring him a beer. "Hate to disappoint you, buddy," he told Seb, "but you're not skipping out early today. I need your help."

"On what?"

"I need to get hold of Eric's computer. He had use of one at the office, right?"

"Of course he did. He was the vice president of Accounting. But why do you need his computer?"

The bartender set a napkin and a beer in front of Rob. Rob nodded his thanks before turning his attention back to Seb. "To see if he kept any kind of personal files on it. I went by the police department to request access to his home computer, but they'd already sent it to Dallas for analysis."

Seb frowned for a moment, then lifted a shoulder. "I don't know what you'll find, but you're welcome to it. Might take me a while to locate it, though."

"What do you mean?" Rob asked, fearing he'd hit yet another dead end. "I *need* that computer."

Rearing back, Seb gave Rob's shoulder a comforting pat. "Calm down, Sherlock. The computer's at Wescott Oil…somewhere. It's just that I had Eric's office cleaned out and new equipment installed before the new vice president of Accounting I named moved in."

"So where is the old one?" Rob asked in growing frustration.

Seb shrugged. "Beats the hell out of me. But my inventory clerk will know. I'll check with him first thing Monday morning and give you a call when it's located."

"Monday morning!" Rob echoed. "But I need that computer *now.*"

Seb glanced at his watch. "It's already after five. Jim will be long gone by now."

Rob tried his best to temper his frustration. "Couldn't you give him a call and ask him to come back to the office?"

"He lives in Midland," Seb informed him drolly.

"More than an hour away. Probably hasn't even made it home yet. By the time I could get hold of him and he made the drive back, it would be eight or later." He shook his head and reached over to give Rob another pat on the shoulder. "Don't worry, Sherlock. That computer isn't going anywhere. I'll have it for you first thing Monday morning, and that's a promise."

Not anywhere near comforted by the reassurance, Rob grumbled, "Yeah, first thing."

Chuckling, Seb shoved his empty glass across the bar and stood. "Come on. I'll buy you dinner."

Rob drained his beer and pushed from the bar. "Damn right you're buying. I bought yours the last—" He stopped and slapped a hand against his forehead. "Damn! I can't. I'm already late."

"For what?" Seb waggled his brows. "Hot date?"

"Yeah. No." Rob swore again. "I was supposed to meet Rebecca Todman at my place at five-thirty." He punched Seb on the arm as he hurried past him. "But you still owe me a dinner," he called over his shoulder.

As Rob drove up to his house, he breathed a sigh of relief when he saw that Rebecca's van was still parked out front. He'd feared that she'd already given up on him and left. He shut off the ignition and coasted around back, while scanning the house and yard for a sign of her.

He caught a flash of blue beneath the oak tree that shaded his breakfast room and patio, and focused on it, recognizing it as the same pastel blue of a shirt he'd seen her wearing at her shop. He braked and just sat there for a moment, watching as she stretched to her toes to hang a birdhouse from one of the tree's lower limbs. Looking pleased with herself, she sank back down to her heels and dusted off her hands. She turned her wrist to glance at her watch. Whatever pleasure hanging the birdhouse had given her slowly melted from her face.

He could almost hear her sigh of disappointment, almost feel its weight in the droop of her shoulders, the leadenness of her movements as she bent to pick up a hummingbird feeder.

A vise clamped around Rob's chest and squeezed as he watched her move deeper into the tree's shadows, searching for a limb to hang the feeder on. He'd never arrived home to find anyone waiting for him before. Never experienced that swell of pleasure that came with knowing that his arrival was so anxiously anticipated.

Unsure whether he liked the sensation or not, he climbed from his car and reached blindly behind the seat for his briefcase, his gaze fixed on Rebecca. His fingers struck something else, a different texture entirely than that of his briefcase's soft leather, and he glanced back to see what it was. On the carpet lay the pink begonia he'd told Rebecca he was buying for a friend's mother. The plant's blooms were faded now to a dusty pink, its leaves curling and brittle along their edges, the heat in the car's interior and lack of water having taken their toll.

He reached inside and carefully withdrew the plant, examining it as he straightened. It was alive, but barely. A survivor, he thought, guilt stabbing at him for his responsibility for the plant's half-dead state. But then something else struck him. An association of sorts, he supposed, frowning. Like the plant, he had been ignored, abused, yet had survived, in spite of it all.

But not without scars, he realized, glancing Rebecca's way as he recalled her comment about never seeing him smile. And what of her? he asked himself as he watched her struggle to push the spiked end of an iron stake into the ground. How many scars did she carry?

Whatever the number, he told himself, it was more than enough. He headed her way.

"Sorry I'm late."

Rebecca straightened, startled by the sound of Rob's voice. Struck by a sudden attack of nerves, she pushed her hands down her thighs as she watched him duck beneath a low-hanging limb. "No problem. I hope you don't mind, but I went ahead and got started on the exterior—" She stopped, her gaze going to the wilted plant he held. She glanced back up at him in surprise. "But I don't understand. I thought…"

"I know," he said, lifting a shoulder. "I lied. I made up that story because I wanted to see you again, and this," he said, indicating the wilted plant, "seemed the perfect excuse."

Rebecca stared, unable to believe her ears. He had wanted to see her again? Had even fabricated a story about needing a plant for an ailing friend's mother just so that he'd have an excuse to do so?

"I left it in the car," she heard him say, and forced herself to concentrate on his explanation. "Forgot all about it." He thrust the half-dead plant toward her. "Think you can save it?"

Still stunned by his confession, that he'd actually wanted to see her again, Rebecca opened her hands. "Maybe. I don't know." She lifted the plant to study it in the fading light. "There's a little green left yet. I think I can—" She glanced over at Rob and her heart stuttered a beat. There was a softness in his eyes now that she'd never seen there before. A vulnerability? It was silly, ridiculous even, to think a man as strong and independent as Rob Cole would need or want anyone's help, especially Rebecca's, but she couldn't help feeling that, in offering her the plant, he was asking her to save him, as well.

"Yes," she said, with more conviction than the drooping plant warranted. "I'm sure I can."

Rebecca stepped back to appraise their work. "Perfect," she said, then looked up at Rob, anxious to hear his opinion. "What do you think?"

Rob puckered his lips thoughtfully and pretended to study the arrangement of plants and accessories Rebecca had spent the past forty-five minutes arranging and rearranging around the marble ledge surrounding his sunken Jacuzzi tub. "I don't know," he said doubtfully. "Maybe you should move that tallest plant there in the corner about a quarter of an inch to the left."

She started forward and he reached out, laughing, to catch her hand. "I was kidding. It's fine just as it is."

"I can move it," she insisted, critically eyeing the arrangement as he hauled her back to his side.

The fact that she hadn't jumped when he caught her by the hand or tried to pull away from him didn't go unnoticed by Rob. In fact, if he wasn't mistaken, her fingers were even curled around his and she seemed to be holding on. A major breakthrough in their relationship as far as he was concerned. To further test her acceptance of him, he released her hand to drape his arm along her shoulders. "It's fine," he repeated. "I was just pulling your leg."

She angled her head to peer up at him. "You're sure?"

Chuckling, he drew her around to face him and

placed his hands on her shoulders. "Yes, I'm sure. It's perfect just as—"

Whatever he'd been about to say was lost, as he saw her eyes sharpen then glimmer with what looked to him like expectancy. He slid his gaze to her mouth and nearly groaned when her tongue slipped out to slick nervously over her lips. He quickly assessed the distance between them and knew he was one short fall from temptation.

"Rebecca?"

"Y-yes?"

He took a step closer and slid his arms down her back to loop them around her waist. "Are you thinking what I think you're thinking?"

She gulped. "I don't know," she said breathlessly. "What do you think I'm thinking?"

If spoken by someone other than Rebecca, Rob might have taken the response as flirtatious teasing. But he heard the tremble in her voice, felt it against the arms he had wrapped at her waist, and knew she wasn't flirting with him. She was just too unsure of herself to voice her true thoughts.

"That you want me to kiss you," he said. "And if that is what you're thinking," he hurried to add, "then we're thinking the same damn thing, because I was thinking I'd like to kiss you, too."

Before she could offer an argument or duck and run, as he would've expected from her the day before, he lowered his head and touched his mouth to hers. Sweetness was his first thought. Heat was his second. Both wrapped themselves around him and tangled in his mind, urging him to take the kiss deeper, push the heat a little higher.

He did so on a groan.

Rebecca felt the vibration against her lips, nearly wept at the impatient, masculine sound of it. But her urge to weep wasn't because she was afraid of Rob. Her only fear was that he might stop, that he would end the kiss before she had a chance to completely experience it.

She hadn't thought she was ready for this. Had feared that she might not *ever* be ready for intimacy again.

It had been so long since she'd kissed a man, she realized through the fog that shrouded her mind, so long since she'd felt the pressure of one's mouth on hers without the accompanying fear of bodily harm. Felt the warmth of desire curl in her belly instead of the knots of dread at what she knew was to come.

She'd enjoy this, she told herself, *could* enjoy this, and found the courage to lift her hands to twine them around his neck. She wouldn't panic. There was nothing for her to fear. These were Rob's lips on hers. Rob's arms banded around her. Not Earl's.

Even as she told herself this, Rob slid his knee between hers and gently urged her backward until her shoulder blades bumped the tile on the bathroom wall.

The chill in the tiles lanced through her like a knife.

She wanted to ask him to stop, to back up a little and give her some room. But his mouth was closed over hers, preventing speech. She drew her hands down to his chest so that she could ease him away, but he misinterpreted the move and, with a groan, leaned into her, penning her bodily more fully between the unrelenting tiled wall and his equally hard, muscled chest. She couldn't move, couldn't breathe.

Panic streaked up her spine and wrapped itself around her chest, threatening to smother her, as memories of being held similarly by Earl gripped her. Her back hitting the wall with a crack hard enough to snap bone. Her head thrust back cruelly, while a wide, powerful hand squeezed around her throat. Then it was Earl's mouth covering hers. Earl's body that held her penned against the wall. Not Rob's.

And this time Earl was going to kill her, just as he'd always threatened he would do.

Blinded to all but the need for survival, the overwhelming desire to escape, she bit down hard on the mouth covering hers and pushed fiercely at the wall of the chest crushed against hers.

Rob released her immediately and staggered back a step, his breath coming in hard, grabbing gasps, his ears ringing with her scream of "No!" Tasting copper, he dragged the back of his hand across his mouth, then stared in confusion at the blood smeared there, unsure what had happened, what had gone wrong.

But one look back at Rebecca huddled, sobbing, against the wall, and he knew. "Ah, hell," he swore, cursing himself for his own stupidity, and reached for her.

She whimpered and shrank away, drawing her arms over her head.

His gut twisted at the sight. "Rebecca," he said, forcing a calm to his voice he didn't come close to feeling. When her whimpers gave way to heart-wrenching sobs, he eased closer. "Rebecca." When she seemed only to shrink more deeply within herself, he took her hands and drew them down to hold in his.

She flailed at him wildly, her nails scraping across his cheek and neck before he could subdue her again. "Rebecca," he said more firmly. "It's me. Rob." When she continued to fight him, he wrapped his arms around her, penning them between their bodies. "I'm not going to hurt you. I swear I'm not going to hurt you. Just calm down. Okay? I'm not going to hurt you. I promise." He kept one arm gripped tightly around her and freed the other to rub his hand in slow, soothing strokes down her back.

After what seemed like hours, his voice seemed to finally penetrate whatever nightmare held her and she went limp in his arms, the battle—for the moment at least—over.

He continued to hold her until the trembling had stopped.

"You okay?" he asked when he was sure the worst was over.

"Y-yes."

Though he was relieved to hear her make a sound other than that of the terrified scream and heartrending sobs of before, he heard the rawness in it, the embarrassment that a lay a thick layer beneath. He loosened his hold and dipped his head to peer at her. "You sure?"

She nodded, but kept her face averted, refusing to meet his gaze.

Slowly he unwound his arms from around her and took a cautious step back. "Want to tell me what that was all about?"

She sniffed and turned away, snatching a tissue from a box on the vanity. "It was nothing. Just a panic attack. I...I have them sometimes." She mopped at the tears on her face, then blew her nose. "I'm...I'm claustrophobic."

Rob stared over her head at her reflection in the mirror. The swollen eyes, the blotchy face, souvenirs from the so-called panic attack. Claustrophobic? He didn't believe her for a minute.

"Rebecca," he began, prepared to challenge her.

But she was already turning away and darting past him.

"It's late," she said as she hurried for the door. "I need to go. I'll let myself out," she called over her shoulder, all but running now.

And Rob let her go, knowing that if he tried to stop her it would only embarrass her more. He'd give her time to get over her embarrassment, he told himself. Time to deal with what had happened.

But not too much time. A day. Two at the most. If he didn't hear from her by then, he was going after her.

"It was mortifying."

Aware of Rebecca's current state of distress, Andrea tried her best to soothe. "Oh, I doubt it was that bad."

Rebecca shot her friend a withering look over her shoulder. "Trust me. I was there. It was mortifying."

Andrea trailed Rebecca through the shop, trying her best to match Rebecca's agitated pace. "Did you explain to him why you panicked? I'm sure, if you had, he would've understood."

Rebecca stopped so abruptly Andrea had to put up a hand to keep from plowing right through her.

"Explain?" Rebecca repeated, and whirled, her eyes blazing. "I moved to Royal because no one here *knew* about my past. Why on earth do you think I would *tell* someone, especially Rob Cole, that my husband abused me, when I've gone to such lengths to escape all that?"

"It wasn't your fault, Rebecca," Andrea said quietly. "Earl was the guilty party in the relationship, not you."

"It *was* my fault," Rebecca argued. "I stayed, didn't I? I stayed with him for four long years, because I was too big a coward to ask him for a divorce."

"But you *did* ask him for a divorce," Andrea reminded her sternly.

Groaning, Rebecca dropped her face into her hands, seeing again Earl's face when she'd finally found the courage to tell him she was leaving him. The rage that had twisted his features, the blood-red flush that had masked his perfect tan.

"Yes," she mumbled, her reply muffled further by her hands. She dropped them and slowly lifted her head, her eyes dull with the life that Earl had all but beaten out of her. "But I'll never know if I would have been able to go through with it, will I? Earl fixed that by dying in the car wreck."

"So what if he did?" Andrea asked impatiently. "You took a stand and refused to let him control you any longer. And you've taken several more since."

Rebecca sank onto a stool behind the register, her energy drained by the emotional display. "Name one," she said wearily.

"You stood up to your in-laws when they contested your rights to Earl's estate."

"I didn't. My lawyer did."

Ignoring her, Andrea continued, ticking off the items on her fingers. "You moved to a strange town where you knew no one. You bought a house. Opened a business. And you—"

Rebecca held up a hand, stopping her friend before she could go on. "I did those things for me, not to take a stand against Earl or anyone else."

"Exactly," Andrea replied, without missing a beat. "And that's what this is all about. *You*. Rebecca Todman. Doing things for yourself because *you* want to do them, not because someone else wants or expects it of you. And thumbing your nose at those who don't approve of your choices, while you're doing them,'' she added proudly.

''Thumbing my nose?'' Rebecca snorted a laugh. ''Yeah. That's me, all right. I'm a real tough broad.''

Andrea dropped onto the stool next to Rebecca's. ''Well, you can laugh if you want,'' she said with a stubborn lift of her chin, ''but you *have* come a long way. You aren't the meek little mouse that Earl liked to use as a punching bag anymore.''

Rebecca's face paled. ''I was, wasn't I?''

Regretting the thoughtless comparison, Andrea slipped an arm around Rebecca's shoulder. ''I didn't mean that literally. But you have changed, Rebecca. You're more independent now, more in control than you ever were when you were with Earl.''

''Judging from what happened last night, I'd say I've got a long way to go yet.''

Andrea withdrew her arm to pat Rebecca's knee. ''You'll get there. You'll see. But first you've got to accept the fact that all men aren't like Earl. Specifically, Rob.''

Rebecca dropped her elbows to her knees and her face to her hands. ''Oh, God,'' she moaned miserably. ''I'll never be able to face him again. I can't.''

''You will because you have to,'' Andrea replied in that matter-of-fact way of hers. ''It's just another step in freeing yourself of your past.''

Rebecca angled her head to frown at Andrea. ''Easy for you to say. You weren't the one who hyperventilated over a simple little kiss.''

''Simple?'' Andrea repeated, lifting a brow. ''Rob Cole's kisses are anything but simple.''

Rebecca straightened slowly, suddenly feeling sick. ''I had no idea that you and Rob had been…involved.''

Andrea dismissed Rebecca's assumption with a careless wave. "Don't worry. The only relationship Rob and I have ever had is one of friendship." She cut a sly glance at Rebecca. "But women *do* talk, you know. And from what I've heard, Rob is an excellent kisser. Among other things," she added, then laughed when Rebecca shot off her stool, her cheeks flaming a bright red.

Five

Prior to that morning, Rebecca had thought she'd known what dread meant. But as the day wore on, she learned the true meaning of the word. She discovered it was something alive that crawled just beneath her skin, a lead ball and chain shackled to her ankle that dragged at her with each weighty step. A gnarled finger that gleefully pushed the hands on the wall clock faster toward closing time, then pointed at her, mocking her fear of seeing Rob again.

A hundred times or more she picked up the phone to call him and tell him she couldn't complete the job, knowing she'd never be able to face him again. Not after making such a fool of herself. But each time she replaced the phone, without ever making the call. She'd have to finish the job, she told herself miserably. She could ill afford the loss of revenue or the black mark against her business's good name if she backed out now.

After locking up for the day, she climbed into her van and drove to his ranch, reconciled to the humiliation that awaited her. But when she arrived, she didn't see a sign of Rob, or his car. Sending up a silent prayer of thanks, she quickly unloaded her tools and went to work, hoping to finish the initial layout of the beds so she could leave before he returned.

She'd managed to mark the borders on both sides of the walk and had begun to turn the soil in one when she heard the sound of an engine. Sure that it was Rob returning, she braced herself, then stole a glance over her shoulder.

But instead of Rob's sleek sports car, a truck pulling a trailer was barreling toward the house, kicking up a swirling column of dust behind it. With a screech of brakes, the truck stopped in front of the house and the driver stuck his head out the window.

"Hey!" he yelled. "Rob home?"

Rebecca placed a hand on her brow, shading her eyes against the late-afternoon sun, but didn't recognize the man behind the wheel. "No, but I expect him any time now."

He spat a stream of tobacco juice out the window, grumbled something under his breath, then yelled, "I ain't got time to wait. Hightail it on down to the barn and sign the paperwork for me, while I unload."

Before Rebecca could explain that she didn't have the authority to sign anything for Rob, the man ducked his head back inside and drove off.

Stunned by his rudeness, she stared after him. *The nerve,* she thought furiously, then threw down her hoe and marched after him.

"Listen, mister," she began as she approached the rear of the trailer, ready to give him a piece of her mind. "I—" She jumped back out of the way to keep from being run over when the man hopped down from the trailer almost on top of her, leading a horse behind him. She watched the horse sway past her on unsteady legs, its head hanging low, its ribs sticking out so far she could have plucked a song from its bones.

"Oh, my heavens," she murmured, staring in horror at the emaciated beast. She ran to catch up with the man, who was already entering the barn. "What's wrong with this horse? Is it sick? Why are you bringing it here? Does Rob know you're doing this? Oh, you poor thing," she said tearfully, reaching to touch a tentative hand to one of the horse's protruding ribs.

Oblivious to her concern for the horse, the old man slipped the halter over the animal's head and gave it a slap on the rump, urging it into a stall. He secured the gate, then turned, working a fat chaw of tobacco to the opposite side of his mouth as he pulled a folded paper from his shirt pocket. He shoved it at her, along with a pen. "Sign right here."

Rebecca backed up a step. "I can't sign that. I don't have the authority."

Scowling, the man spat a stream of tobacco juice onto the ground between Rebecca's feet. "You ain't buyin' the horse, lady. You're jist verifyin' that I delivered it."

He pushed the pen and paper at her again. "Now, sign on the bottom line, so I can get on home and eat my dinner before my old lady feeds it to the dogs."

She tucked her hands behind her back. "I can't."

He narrowed his eyes at her, as if he thought he could intimidate her into signing.

Rebecca stubbornly lifted her chin.

Scowling, he gave his pants a hitch. "All right. Suit yourself. Makes me no never mind one way or t'other. I'll just load the old nag back up and take her to the glue factory. That's where I shoulda taken her in the first place."

Rebecca snatched the paper from his hand before he could stuff it back into his pocket. "You certainly will not!" She quickly scrawled her name across the bottom of the paper. "The very idea," she muttered darkly, then stopped, her eyes widening when she saw the dollar amount listed on the invoice. "Why, this is highway robbery," she cried. "That horse can't possibly be worth this much money."

He spat again, this time missing the tip of her shoe by centimeters. "The glue factory will pay that and more." He plucked the invoice from her hand and crammed it into his shirt pocket. "Tell Rob I've got another one for him," he called over his shoulder as he turned to leave. "Supposed to pick it up in a couple of days."

Her lips pursed, Rebecca watched the old man climb back into his truck and drive away. As an afterthought she yelled after him, "Tell him yourself! I'm not your secretary." But he didn't hear her. Or pretended not to. The man was so ornery, she wouldn't have put it past him if he *had* heard her pithy remark and chosen to ignore both it and her.

But she was rather proud of herself for finding the courage to make it.

Rob signaled the bartender to bring him a beer, then joined some other members of the Texas Cattleman's Club already seated at a table.

"Hey, Rob," said Keith Owens, a high-powered businessman and computer expert, as Rob pulled up a chair to join them. "How's it going?"

Rob lifted a shoulder, then mumbled his thanks to the bartender who set his beer in front of him. "All right, I guess."

Keith leaned closer, peering at Rob's face. "Whoa. What happened to you? You try to break up a cat fight or something?"

Rob touched a finger to the cut on his lip where Rebecca had bitten him, then shook his head, heat crawling up his neck. "No. It's just a little cut, is all."

"I'll bet it was a woman," Jason said. "Rob likes his women a little wild in bed. Right, Rob?"

Rob shot Jason a look that would peel paint off a wall. "Drop it, would you? I said it's nothing. Just a little scratch." He took a drink of his beer, then looked around, hoping to change the subject. "Where's Seb? I thought I'd find him here."

Dorian, Seb's half brother and a new member of the club, shook his head. "Haven't seen him. Guess he's lying low for a while."

Instantly alert, Rob glanced at Dorian. "Lying low? Why?"

Dorian shrugged. "The murder investigation. I think it's beginning to get to him."

Rob frowned, frustrated by his own lack of progress with the case. "I know he's anxious to have Eric's murderer behind bars, but that's going to take some time. With no leads, no evidence." He huffed a breath. "Hell, we haven't got anything to go on."

"That's just it," Dorian replied. "The police are beginning to lean on Seb. Asking him a lot a questions that he refuses to answer." He shook his head again, then sank back, blowing out a breath. "I have to say

I'm worried about him. If he'd just tell the police where he was the night of Eric's murder, they'd get off his back.''

Stunned, Rob stared. He was unaware that Seb had become a suspect in the case. "The police think Seb's responsible for Eric's murder?"

"Looks that way," Dorian replied miserably. "As you just said, they don't have any leads, no evidence. I think they're anxious to close the case, and Seb's going to be their fall guy." He glanced around the table, then added, "They're questioning a lot of Wescott employees. Personally, I'm glad that I have an alibi for that night. I was at the diner, having a late dinner, the night Eric was murdered. Laura Edwards was my waitress and can verify that I was there."

Laura Edwards? Rob remembered the waitress from the afternoon that she'd waited on him and Rebecca, and the stricken look on her face when she'd overheard them discussing Eric's murder. Giving himself a mental shake, he forced himself to listen to Dorian.

"Seb, on the other hand—" Dorian shook his head. "And he sure isn't helping his case any with the way he's been acting."

"What do you mean?" Rob asked.

Dorian frowned, then shook his head again. "I don't know, really. He's just acting strange. Kind of secretive. Won't talk to anybody about the murder. Not even me."

Rob rose, having heard enough. "He'll talk to me."

But Rob didn't talk to Seb that afternoon. He never found him. Not at his office, not at his house.

On his way home, Rob cruised by the Texas Cattleman's Club one last time, just to see if Seb had showed up, but didn't see his car in the parking lot.

By the time he arrived at his ranch, it was after dark. He was surprised to find Rebecca's van parked out front. After the emotional display the night before, he really hadn't expected to see her again so soon. Not without him making the first move.

But he was even more surprised when, after a quick look around, he *didn't* find Rebecca.

Wondering where she'd gotten to, he walked around the house to the back, but didn't find a sign of her there, either. He'd just turned to retrace his steps when he noticed the barn light on.

Curious, he headed that way.

He heard her before he saw her. Her voice held the soft, soothing lilt of a mother comforting a sick child. Mesmerized by the sound, he followed it to a far stall. And there he found Rebecca feeding fistfuls of grass to a skeleton of a horse.

He could only stare.

"Rob will know what to do," he heard her tell the horse. "Just hang on a little longer. Okay?"

The horse tossed its head, as if it understood, and Rebecca smiled. "You're smart, aren't you, girl?" she murmured, rubbing the horse's muzzle. "Smarter than that crotchety old man who brought you here."

"Who?" Rob asked. "Fegan?"

Startled, Rebecca glanced up, then laid a hand over her heart. "Oh, thank goodness, you're here," she said in relief. "The most disagreeable old man just dumped this horse here and left." She looked back at the animal and wrung her hands. "I didn't know what to do, what to feed her, and I was so afraid that she'd die before you came home."

Rob opened the gate and stepped inside, shutting the gate behind him. "Looks to me like you're both doing just fine. Though I do have hay,'' he added, noting the small pile of grass heaped at her feet, grass he figured she must have picked from his pasture. He scratched the animal between its ears, then tipped up its head, examining first its eyes, then its teeth. ''She's an old one. Twenty-four, if she's a day.''

''He made me sign a paper before he'd leave her,'' she told him, her anger with the tobacco-spitting old man making her voice sharp. ''I told him I couldn't, that I didn't have the authority to sign for you. But he said he was going to take her to the glue factory if I didn't.''

Out of the corner of his eye Rob noticed that she'd quit wringing her hands and had balled them into fists at her sides. So there was some fire in the lady, he noted, just as he'd suspected. Good for her.

''Probably would have, too,'' he replied. He gave the horse a comforting pat, then gave Rebecca's shoulder one as he passed by her. ''You did the right thing.''

She turned to stare after him as he opened the gate. ''I did?''

''Yep. You did.''

He latched the gate and strode away.

Rebecca bolted after him. ''Wait!'' she cried, her fingers fumbling with the latch in her haste. ''Where are you going? You can't just leave me here with her. She needs— That's just it,'' she wailed, near tears. ''I don't know what she needs!'' She managed to throw open the gate, and looked frantically around for Rob. She spotted him just as he passed through an open doorway at the opposite end of the barn. She took off after him.

Breathless, she skidded to a stop just inside the room. Rob stood before an open refrigerator opposite her, calmly filling a syringe. Her stomach did a slow, nauseating flip.

"What are you doing?" she whispered. "You aren't going to put her down, are you?" She ran to grab his arm. "You can't! I won't let you. I know she's old and sick, but she isn't ready to die yet. I'm sure she's not."

He shook free and frowned at her. "I'm not putting her down. I'm just giving her a shot."

Rebecca sucked in a breath, seeing for the first time the cut on his lip, the jagged red line across his cheek. She'd done that to him, she realized, and swallowed back the nausea that rose. With her teeth, with her nails. She'd been so concerned about the horse, she hadn't really looked at Rob's face before.

Regretting the pain she must have inflicted, she lifted a tentative hand to touch the scratch. She gasped, flinching, when he grabbed her wrist before she could.

"What?" he snapped impatiently, shoving her hand away.

She drew it behind her back. "Your face. I did that. I'm sorry. I didn't mean to hurt—"

He waved away her apology. "It's nothing."

"Oh, but it is. And I'm sorry. Truly I am."

Scowling, he caught her elbow. "Believe me, I've had worse. Now, come on. I need to give the horse a shot of penicillin."

Rebecca had to jog to match his pace or be dragged along at his side. "You know how to do that?"

"I've done it a time or two." He stopped at the gate and released her to open it. "It may be too late," he said, moving to the mare's side to run a hand along her neck. Flattening his lips, he shook his head. "I don't know. We'll just have to wait and see." He motioned for Rebecca to draw closer. "Hold her head while I give her the shot."

Swallowing hard, Rebecca nodded and eased to stand at the horse's head. She looped an arm over the animal's neck and drew its head down to rest over her shoulder. "It's okay, girl," she soothed, watching as Rob prepared to make the injection. "You'll just feel a little prick, that's all. Tomorrow you'll feel a whole lot better. You'll see." Her gaze met Rob's and she saw the doubt in his eyes. "She will," she said stubbornly, then winced as he pushed the needle into the horse's hide. She felt the horse jerk instinctively, and tightened her hold. "She will," she repeated. "She has to."

"You're sure it's okay to leave her?"

Rob pulled Rebecca along with him. "Yes, I'm sure."

"But what if she needs something?" she fretted, looking back over her shoulder at the barn.

With a frustrated sigh, Rob stopped on the patio and pulled Rebecca around to face him. Planting his hands on her shoulders, he placed his face even with hers. "Look," he said patiently, "we've given her antibiotics, food, water and a clean bed of hay to sleep on. There's nothing more we can do. The rest is up to her."

"But…"

He pressed his hands against her shoulders, forcing her down onto one of the chairs circling the patio table. He bent forward, bracing his hands on his knees, his eyes level with hers. "Now, you can sit right here and keep an eye on the barn, if that's what makes you happy, but I'm going inside to get us something to eat. I, for one, haven't eaten dinner, and I'm starving."

Her gaze fixed worriedly on the barn, she lifted a

hand and waved him toward the house. "Nothing for me. But get yourself something, if you like. I'll just stay here and keep watch."

With a rueful shake of his head, Rob went inside. He returned minutes later with two bottles of beer caught between his fingers and balancing a plate with his other hand. He set the plate on the table, then twisted the cap off one of the beers and stuck it in front of Rebecca's face. "Thirsty?"

She strained to see around the bottle, and pushed it away. "No, thanks."

He rolled his eyes and caught her hand, forcing her fingers around the bottle. "Drink," he ordered.

She did as instructed, but Rob was sure she wasn't even aware of doing so. Her attention was fixed on the barn.

He dropped down on the chair next to hers. "Hungry?"

"Uh-uh."

He plucked a wedge of cantaloupe from the tray, popped it into his mouth and settled back to watch her watch the barn. Her attention was so riveted on the building and the sick horse inside, he was sure she wasn't even aware of his presence. To test his theory, he said, "I sure would like to take you to bed."

She responded with a distracted "Mmm-hmm."

Rob choked on a laugh and picked up another piece of cantaloupe. He leaned toward her and pressed it to her lips. She opened her mouth without even looking at him, rolled her lips over the fruit and drew it inside.

He sank back and watched the slow movements of her jaw as she chewed, wondering why he found that simple act such a turn-on. The longer he watched, the more he found himself wishing that her "mmm-hmm" had been an affirmative response, instead of a distracted one, and given while in full control of her mental faculties. He'd like nothing more than to take her to bed right now and make love with her for about six hours straight. And that was something, considering she'd fought him like a wild woman after only a kiss.

"Rebecca?"

When she didn't respond, he firmed his voice. "Rebecca."

She glanced his way and slowly drew him into focus, as if coming out of a trance. "Yes?"

Scowling, he took a sip of his beer, then gestured with it at the tray. "Eat something."

She turned her gaze back to the barn. "No, thank you. I'm really not hungry."

With a huff of breath, he plucked another piece of the juicy cantaloupe from the tray and popped it into his mouth. Sucking the juice from the sweet fruit, he mentally patted himself on the back for taking the time to stop at the neighbor kid's produce stand. He figured the fifty-dollar bill he'd handed the kid in exchange for the cantaloupe was money well spent. Rob wouldn't starve and the kid's mother could put the cash toward her husband's outstanding medical bills. An even trade, as far as Rob was concerned.

While he was congratulating himself for stopping to make the purchase, Rebecca kept watch, her ears tuned for any sound of distress. A whinny from the pasture drew her gaze from the barn. She squinted through the darkness, counting one, two, three, four horses? There were more, she knew, because she remembered seeing a sizable herd that first day she'd toured Rob's home. Though she hadn't seen the horses up close, not one of

DIANA PALMER

MERCENARY'S WOMAN
SOLDIERS OF FORTUNE

We'd like to send you **2 FREE** books and a surprise gift to introduce you to Silhouette Desire®. Accept our special offer today and

Get Ready for a totally Refreshing Experience!

HOW TO QUALIFY:

1. With a coin, carefully scratch off the silver area on the card at right to see what we have for you—2 FREE BOOKS and a FREE GIFT—ALL YOURS! ALL FREE!

2. Send back the card and you'll receive two brand-new Silhouette Desire® novels. These books have a cover price of $3.99 each in the U.S. and $4.50 each in Canada, but they are yours to keep absolutely free!

3. There's no catch. You're under no obligation to buy anything. We charge nothing—ZERO—for your first shipment and you don't have to make any minimum number of purchases—not even one!

4. The fact is, thousands of readers enjoy receiving books by mail from the Silhouette Reader Service®. They enjoy the convenience of home delivery…they like getting the best new novels at discount prices, BEFORE they're available in stores…and they love their *Heart to Heart* subscriber newsletter featuring author news, horoscopes, recipes, book reviews and much more!

5. We hope that after receiving your free books you'll want to remain a subscriber. But the choice is yours—to continue or cancel, any time at all. So why not take us up on our invitation with no risk of any kind. You'll be glad you did!

SPECIAL FREE GIFT!

We can't tell you what it is…but we're sure you'll like it! A FREE gift just for giving the Silhouette Reader Service® a try!

Visit us at
www.eHarlequin.com

The **2 FREE BOOKS** we send you will be selected from **SILHOUETTE DESIRE®**, the series that brings you...highly passionate, powerful and provocative reads.

Books received may vary.

Scratch off the silver area to see what the Silhouette Reader Service has for you.

V *Silhouette®*
Where love comes alive™

YES! I have scratched off the silver area above. Please send me the **2 FREE** books and gift for which I qualify. I understand I am under no obligation to purchase any books, as explained on the back and on the opposite page.

326 SDL DH49   225 SDL DH47

FIRST NAME	LAST NAME

ADDRESS

APT.#	CITY

STATE/PROV.	ZIP/POSTAL CODE

them had appeared in the emaciated condition of the horse currently stalled in the barn.

So why had he bought a horse so obviously near death? she wondered, then turned to him.

"Why did that man bring that horse here?"

Rob's hand froze inches from his mouth. He forced himself to pop the cantaloupe inside, chewed, then chased it down with a swig of beer, hoping she wouldn't press him for an answer.

"Why?" she repeated.

Stalling for time, he wiped his hands down his thighs, removing the juice, and tried to come up with a reasonable excuse to offer her. One other than the truth. Unable to do so, he replied vaguely, "He brings me horses every now and then."

She shifted on her chair to fully face him. "But why? The horse is old and obviously in poor health. Why would you want an animal in such bad condition, when you could just as easily buy a healthy one?"

Irritated by her prodding, Rob pushed to his feet and crossed to the edge of the patio. He took a drink of his beer, then gestured with it at the barn. "Why not?" he replied carelessly. "We've all got our eccentricities. Mine just happens to be that I like old horses."

Rebecca rose slowly and crossed to stand beside him. She stared at the barn, struggling to put the confusing pieces of the puzzle together. She looked up at him, her eyes narrowed in suspicion. "How many horses like this one have you given a home?"

He shrugged, but wouldn't look at her. "I don't know. A few, maybe."

"A few," she repeated, thinking of the herd of horses she'd seen and wondering what condition they had arrived in. A swell of emotion rose in her throat as she stared at his stubborn profile, realizing she'd been right about him. Rob Cole did have a tender heart. She turned her gaze to the barn again. "That's really kind of you."

He snorted and took another swig of his beer. "I'm a lot of things, but kind certainly isn't one of them."

"In your opinion."

"In *anyone's* opinion. Just ask around town. Everybody will tell you same damn thing. The Coles are a mean breed of men."

"Only because you want them to think you are."

He looked at her then, his eyes dark with fury, his face taut with it. "What do you know about anything? You've been in Royal, what? Six months?"

To her amazement, his anger didn't frighten her. Not this time. Not now that she'd discovered how truly kind and generous he was. "Yes. But whether I'd been here six months or six years, I would still think the same thing of you."

"You wouldn't if you'd known my father."

"I don't have to know the father to know the son. You are two entirely different people."

"Blood's the same," he argued stubbornly. "And the Cole blood runs toward mean."

"I've known mean," she said in a voice so quiet, he had to strain to hear her. "And you haven't got what it takes."

The sincerity in her voice, the trust he found in the blue eyes turned up to his, almost made Rob believe that what she said was true, that he'd inherited nothing of his father's meanness.

But then he curled his hand into a fist, felt the strength in it, the power, the anger pulsing through the veins bulging on his arm. Remembered the satisfaction he'd felt when he'd plowed that fist into his father's face. The pleasure he'd experienced when he'd heard bone crack. The lack of any emotion at all when they'd finally pulled him off his father, his hands slick with his father's blood.

Scowling, he turned away from Rebecca. "You can think whatever you want." He tossed the words over his shoulder as he strode to his house. "I'm going to bed."

Rob awakened slowly, his tongue thick, his mouth dry as cotton, his head pounding as if a Fourth of July percussion band was marching around inside. Moaning, he dragged himself from bed and stumbled to the bathroom, holding his throbbing head between his hands. He released his head to twist on the shower faucet, then stepped beneath the spray.

He set his teeth as the first blast of cold water hit him high on the chest, then braced a hand on the wall and ducked his head beneath it. He stood there a good five minutes and let the needlelike spray punish him, waiting for his head to clear. When that didn't seem to do the trick, he straightened and let the water hit him full in the face.

That had the desired effect. Within minutes he was cold-stone sober. Or, at the very least, more sober than when he'd crawled into bed only a few short hours before.

Remembering the reason he'd stayed up half the night, working at getting himself good and drunk, he shut off the water with an angry twist of his hand. He slicked his hands over his hair as he stepped from the shower, and sent droplets of water flying halfway across the room.

Well, she was wrong, he told himself. He wasn't

kind. He was mean. Just like his father. Though Rob had learned to keep a tight rein on the meanness, he knew it was there inside him. Lived in fear that it still lurked just beneath the surface, just waiting to bust out.

Though he was sober now, his dark mood stayed with him as he dressed. And when he stepped outside to check on the horse that Fegan had delivered the day before, he didn't even notice the sun's bright glare. The blackness of his soul shadowed everything.

Once inside the barn, he reached automatically for the feed bucket hanging on the wall, nabbed it in his right hand as he strode by. At the oat bin he stopped to fill the bucket, then walked on to the stall. With his gaze moving instinctively over the horse, checking for any change in her condition, he opened the gate and stepped inside. "Hey, girl," he murmured, letting the horse dip her head into the bucket while he gave her a more thorough inspection. "You're looking a whole lot better this morning."

He caught a movement out of his peripheral vision and spun just as Rebecca pushed to her elbows from the stall floor. Bits of hay clung to her hair and shirt and an old army blanket wrapped her legs.

She blinked up at him sleepily. "What time is it?"

Rob stared, the early-morning huskiness in her voice tying his tongue in a knot, while another swelled in his groin.

She didn't seem to notice, but kicked free of the blanket and pushed to her feet. "Oh-h-h-h" she moaned, lifting her arms high. "I'm really stiff." She made a purring sound deep in her throat as she stretched her fingertips toward the ceiling, lengthening her cramped muscles.

He slid his gaze down to where her breasts strained

against the buttons of her wrinkled cotton blouse. Lower to where her belly button peeked from the gap the stretch created between shirt and slacks. That knot in his groin cinched tighter.

She dropped her arms, gave them a shake, then turned her wrist to glance at her watch. She looked over at Rob in surprise. "I had no idea it was so late. She's okay, isn't she?" she asked, obviously responding to his stricken look.

He opened his mouth to answer, but couldn't push a word beyond his paralyzed throat.

Her face creased with concern, she hurried to the horse and placed a hand beneath her forelock, as if testing for a temperature. She glanced at Rob again. "She *is* okay, isn't she?"

"Yeah," he said, then cleared his throat, relieved to find that he'd recovered his voice. "Much better."

Her smile was instantaneous, dazzling, and chased the darkness that wanted to claim Rob's soul back into the shadows.

"Good." She stooped and picked up the blanket she'd wrapped herself in. "I'll just put this back in the tack room, then I'll get out of your way."

Rob watched her, his heart clenching at the thought of her leaving. Last night he'd have paid her to leave. But now...

"Wait!"

She stopped and looked back at him curiously.

He racked his mind, trying to think of a way to delay her departure. The obvious one stood at his side. He forced some of the panic from his shoulders and laid a hand on the horse's swayed back. "I could use your help giving her another injection. If you can spare the time, that is."

She tossed the blanket over the stall gate. "No problem. I wasn't planning on leaving just yet, anyway. Since I'm here, I thought I'd work on the flower beds for a while before I headed home."

"That's even better," he said, and offered her one of his rare smiles. "Being as this is Sunday, I've got the day free and can give you a hand."

Rebecca knelt in the freshly tilled soil along the gentle curve of the walkway, carefully patting soil over the roots of the lavender plant she'd just placed in a hole. While she worked, the sun shone warmly on her back, birds serenaded from high in the trees and the scent of lavender filled the air.

Rebecca couldn't remember ever feeling more content, more relaxed.

Which was amazing, she realized, glancing over to look at Rob where he worked on the opposite side of the walkway with a spade, turning the soil. Dressed in worn work boots, faded jeans and a chambray shirt, its tails flapping in the soft breeze, he looked like a migrant farm worker. Sweat dripped from his chin and soaked his shirt in darker blotches of blue on both his chest and back. The cap he wore had a dark ring of sweat around it and his hair curled in damp clumps along his neck. Dirt lined the creases on his face and a streak of it smeared one cheek, where he'd dragged the back of his hand across it, wiping away sweat.

Rebecca was sure there wasn't a more handsome man anywhere in the world.

He glanced up and caught her looking at him. He lifted a brow in question. "Need a break?"

She smiled and shook her head. "Only if you do."

He stabbed the spade into the soil and peeled off his

cap. With a sigh, he crooked his elbow and dragged it across his forehead. "I could use something wet to drink. I'm just about parched."

Laughing, she pushed to her feet. "How about if I make us some tea?"

He slapped the cap back over his head and tugged it down to shade his eyes. "Sounds good to me."

They walked around back together and entered his house through the kitchen door. While Rob searched the pantry for tea bags, Rebecca washed her hands, then put on a kettle to boil.

He tossed a box of tea bags onto the counter, set out a pitcher, then crossed to the sink, turned on the water and stuck his head beneath the tap. He came up with a growl, shaking his head like a dog.

She bit back a smile as she watched him. "You don't have to help me. I certainly don't expect you to."

He grabbed a kitchen towel and wiped it down his face, then rubbed it over his head as he crossed to the table. "Never said you did. But I enjoy a little physical labor every now and then." He dropped onto the chair with a groan and let his head fall back, his eyes close.

She poured the water over the tea bags and joined him at the table while it steeped. "What you've done this morning is more than a little," she reminded him.

He lifted his head and opened one eye to peer at her. "Do you hear me complaining?"

She laughed at his sour expression. "Not in so many words, but you look beat."

Scowling, he closed his eye and let his head fall back again. "Yeah. And you look fresh enough to run a marathon."

Rebecca glanced down at her wrinkled shirt and

soiled slacks. "I look as if I slept in my clothes. Which I did," she added with a chuckle.

He lifted his head to peer at her again. This time through both eyes. "Why'd you sleep in the barn, anyway?"

She shrugged, suddenly self-conscious. "I didn't want to leave the horse all alone. Not that I would have known what to do if there had been a change in her condition," she added.

"You gave her what she needed. Attention," he said, responding to her quizzical look. "That's what she was suffering from more than anything. Lack of attention."

Reminded of the horse's weak and malnourished condition, she braced her arms on the table and leaned toward him. "What happened to her? Where did she come from?"

Rob straightened and picked up the towel to wipe it across his face. "I don't know where she came from. Fegan finds them and brings them out here. As to what happened to her, I can only guess."

"What?" she asked.

He lifted a shoulder and drew the towel between his hands. Finding a loose thread, he plucked at it. "Sometimes when a horse gets that old and can't earn its keep any longer, the owner will quit feeding it, leaving it up to the animal to forage for food on its own. Sometimes the animal is physically abused for one reason or another."

"But why would anyone abuse an animal that they've purchased? Why not just sell it to someone else who would care for it properly?"

He glanced up, his expression grim. "Because some people are just plain mean. They'll tie a horse up where it can't defend itself and beat it, just for the hell of it.

They'll use a whip on it, a length of barbed wire, sometimes a board." He dropped his gaze to the towel again, scowling, and muttered, "Sometimes they use their hands."

Rebecca gulped, knowing what kind of pain a man's hand could inflict. "And you buy them," she said quietly. "Feed them, care for them and give them a home."

He pushed to his feet. "Like I said, I like old horses."

Rebecca watched him stride to the refrigerator and jerk open the door. It was more than a whim that compelled him to buy sick and abused horses, she realized slowly. But what? she asked herself. What would motivate a man to do such a kind and generous thing, when he obviously stood to gain nothing for his efforts?

Convinced by the tension in his shoulders that he wouldn't welcome any more of her questions, especially any aimed at the motives behind his acts of kindness, she rose and made the tea.

"Would you mind filling the glasses with ice?" she asked, hoping to draw him from the refrigerator, where he seemed to be hiding. "The tea is just about ready."

Six

————

"**D**o you know Rob very well?"

Hunched over the counter watching Rebecca put together a decorative basket, Andrea raised an eyebrow as she passed her a small pot of ivy. "As well as anyone, I suppose. Why?"

Rebecca hesitated, not wanting to place Andrea in an awkward position by asking her questions about Rob's personal life. "It's nothing, really," she said as she tucked the pot among the others she'd already placed in the basket. "It's just that while I was working there this past weekend, a man delivered an old, sick horse to his ranch. I told Rob how kind I thought he was for giving the horse a home and it seemed to anger him. In fact, he insisted he wasn't kind, he was mean, and that meanness ran in his family."

When Andrea didn't immediately respond, Rebecca glanced up. Seeing the frown on her friend's face, she waved away the question. "Never mind. It's none of my business. It just struck me as such an odd thing for him to say."

"Odd, maybe," Andrea said, her tone grim, "but true. At least, the part about meanness running in his family. Rob's the exception, though he tries very hard to make people believe otherwise. His father, on the other hand…"

Rebecca motioned for Andrea to pass her another plant. "What?" she asked, her curiosity aroused.

Andrea nudged a finger through the remaining pots, selected one and passed it to Rebecca. "Mean to the bone. Cruel, even, from what I've heard. He raised horses, both for the track and for private sell." She shuddered. "I've heard stories of things that man did that would curdle your blood."

Rebecca pushed aside the basket to give Andrea her full attention. "Tell me."

"Now, this is all secondhand," Andrea reminded her. "I don't know for a fact that any of it's true. Though from the number of incidents, I'd have to say there must be some truth in it. Where's there's smoke, there's usually fire," she said sagely.

"Go on," Rebecca urged.

"Well, for instance, there was the time a local vet was called out to their place to tend an injured horse. When he returned to town, he was fit to be tied. According to him, one of the trainers was trying to load a horse into the starting gate for a practice run on the track, and the horse balked, refusing to go in. Rob's father was watching from the rail, and shouting orders. He always carried a bull whip. Some said he even slept with it.

"Anyway, when the horse still refused to enter the

gate, Rob's father jumped the fence, jerked the trainer down from the horse and took the bull whip to the animal. The vet said he'd never seen such a bloody mess in his life. The vet did what he could, but, according to him, the horse was scarred for life and would never run again. After that he refused to treat any more of Mr. Cole's livestock.

"There was another incident," she went on, "where a horse died at their place. A high-powered stud, whose services were considered gold. Rob's father was in debt up to his eyeballs at the time, and it was rumored that he killed the horse to collect the insurance money."

"Did he?"

Andrea shrugged. "No one ever knew for sure. Supposedly the horse went crazy one night during a thunderstorm and kicked down his stall door. He cut his leg so badly on one of the iron rollers attached to the door that he bled to death before the accident was discovered."

"That's possible, isn't it?" Rebecca asked. "I mean, a horse could die from such an injury?"

"Could," Andrea agreed. "But this particular horse had no history of fearing storms or kicking his stall. Or, at least, that's what the groom who cared for him was quoted as saying."

"But wouldn't the groom's testimony be enough to warrant an investigation by the insurance company? Surely they wouldn't pay a claim if there was a question of foul play?"

"Probably not. But the groom disappeared before he could be questioned. Rob's father said the groom was afraid he'd be blamed for the horse's death and ran away to Mexico."

"And did he?" Rebecca asked, hearing the doubt in Andrea's voice.

"Maybe. Who knows? But there were some who suspected that Rob's father killed the groom, to keep him quiet."

Rebecca placed a hand over her stomach, sickened by the thought. "Surely not."

Andrea lifted a shoulder. "Like I said. I don't know whether he did or didn't. I'm just telling you what I heard."

Sobered by the story, Rebecca pulled the basket back in front of her and absently tucked Spanish moss around the base of the plants to conceal the pots. "And Rob?" she asked uneasily. "How does he fit into all this?"

"As far as the death of the horse and the disappearance of the groom goes, he doesn't. He was just a kid when all that happened."

"And his father?" Rebecca asked. "What about him? Does he still raise horses?"

Andrea rose. "Maybe you should ask Rob about his father. I've said more than I should have, as it is." She turned to leave, but stopped and glanced back over her shoulder. "But I will tell you this. Rob's father was guilty of a lot more than mistreating his livestock."

Rebecca couldn't get Andrea's parting comment out of her mind. It haunted her throughout the day, making her wonder what her friend had meant in saying that Rob's father was guilty of a lot more than just mistreating his livestock. Guilty of what?

She was still puzzling over the odd comment on the drive out to Rob's ranch that afternoon, after closing her shop.

She didn't stop at the house, as she normally did, but

drove straight to the barn, wanting to check on the horse before beginning her work.

Gathering the sack of carrots she'd brought along, she hopped down from her van and strolled into the barn.

"Hey, girl," she said softly as she approached the stall. "How are you doing today?"

The horse stretched its head over the stall door and nudged its nose at the sack she held.

Laughing, Rebecca opened it and pulled out a carrot. "Well, there's definitely nothing wrong with your sense of smell." She offered the horse the carrot, then leapt back with a shriek when the animal nearly took one of her fingers, as well.

"Did she bite you?"

She turned to find that Rob had entered the barn and was striding toward her, his hands fisted at his sides, a dark scowl on his face. The details of the stories Andrea had told her of his father's cruelty leapt to her mind. "No," she said quickly. "Her teeth just grazed my finger. It startled me more than it hurt."

Reaching her, he caught her hand and opened it, spreading her fingers to examine them himself. He poked and prodded, then, having seen for himself that she wasn't injured, he released her. "No harm done."

Rebecca curled her fingers into her palm, her skin tingling from his touch. "No. None at all." *But what about him?* What could have happened to put him in such a dark mood? Gathering her courage, she took a step toward him. "Is something wrong?"

He glanced her way. "No. Why?"

"You look…I don't know. Angry."

He took the sack from her. "Frustrated," he said grimly. "Not angry."

"About what?"

"Not what. Who."

"All right, then, who?"

The creases on his forehead deepened as he drew out a carrot. "It's Sebastian Wescott. He was supposed to have Eric's computer ready for me today, but he never showed up at his office. Doesn't answer his phone, either."

"Do you think something has happened to him?" she asked, thinking of what had happened to Eric.

Rob shook his head. "Seb knows how to take care of himself. He also knows how to hide," he added resentfully, then shook his head again. "He's okay," he told her, and forced a halfhearted smile for her benefit. "He'll surface, when he's ready."

Not wanting to think about what kind of trouble Seb might be in, especially when Rob could do nothing to help his friend until the man decided to make his whereabouts known, Rob held up the carrot. "You feed a horse like this." He demonstrated by laying the carrot on his open palm and offering it to the horse.

"Oh. I see." Rebecca mimicked his actions, holding her hand out flat to the horse this time. She sputtered a laugh at the tickling sensation the animal's velvetlike muzzle created on her skin.

"Tickles, doesn't it?" Grinning, he leaned against the gate and reached to scratch the horse between its ears. "She's looking better today."

"Much," Rebecca agreed, relieved to see that his mood had lightened. When he smiled, he seemed more approachable, less intimidating. Less threatening. She emptied the remaining carrots into the feed trough, then braced her arms on the gate beside his, while they both watched the horse make quick work of the treat.

He nodded toward the animal. "Her appetite's improved, that's for sure. And her eyes are much clearer. She should be ready to be put out in the pasture with the others in another day or two."

As if listening in on the conversation, a horse in the pasture beside the barn whinnied. The mare lifted her head at the sound and whinnied in return.

Rebecca laughed. "She'll like that. I'm sure she gets lonely in here."

"You could always spend the night with her again and keep her company until she's ready to be let out."

She glanced his way, startled by his suggestion, then choked a laugh at the teasing she saw in his eyes. "I don't think my back would survive another night on that hard stall floor."

He slung an arm around her shoulders and drew her away from the gate.

"You could always set up a bed," he suggested. "Although the mare might want to share it with you," he warned. "I know I would."

Rebecca jerked to a stop and looked up at him, unsure if she'd heard him correctly. But the sudden rush of color to his face told her that she hadn't misunderstood. He'd said exactly what she'd thought he'd said.

He dropped his arm from around her. "Sorry," he muttered. "That just slipped out."

Rebecca couldn't think of a thing to say in reply. Gulping, she tore her gaze from his and started walking again, wondering what on earth he could possibly have been thinking for a comment like that to slip out. Was it possible that he really wanted to share a bed with her? Oh, Lord, she thought, her heart pounding at the very thought.

Rob hung back as Rebecca walked on, kicking himself for making such a suggestive comment when he knew damn good and well she had some sort of hang-up about sex. Hadn't he seen a perfect example of that the night he'd kissed her?

He ran to catch up with her. "Rebecca." He caught her arm and pulled her to a stop. "I'm sorry. That was way out of line."

"N-no. It's all right. I just thought..." She pressed her hands to her cheeks. "Oh, I don't know what I thought."

Embarrassed? he asked himself, noting the flush beneath her hands. Or aroused? He decided to take a chance it was the latter. For Rebecca or himself, he wasn't sure, and he wasn't in the mood to examine his motives too closely. If he did, he feared he'd discover his motives in taking the gamble were purely selfish.

He pulled her hands from her cheeks and dipped his head to meet her gaze. "I said I was out of line. And that's true. I was. But what I said was the truth. I would like to share a bed with you. I'm only sorry if I offended you or embarrassed you by saying so."

She shook her head. "You didn't."

A smile curved his mouth at the lie. "Good." He released her hands to drag his slowly up her arms. "There's something between us. I feel it every time I touch you." A shiver shook her and he lifted a brow. "You feel it, too, don't you?"

Rebecca hesitated, uncertain whether to admit to the attraction. "I—I'm not sure what you mean."

"That little jolt to the system. That rush of adrenaline." He rolled his hands over her shoulders, shaping the gentle curves, then pushed his thumbs along the delicate curve of her collarbone. "I feel it. Even now. Don't you?"

"Y-yes. I feel it."

"Does it frighten you?"

"No. Not really."

He stepped closer and let his hands slide down her back. "Scares the hell out of me."

Shocked by his admission, she could only stare.

He chuckled, the sound a low rumble in his chest. "Surprised you, didn't I?"

"Well…yes. You did."

He looped his arms behind her waist and drew her to him, until he was pressed against her, their lips only a whisper away from a kiss. "It does scare me. But only because I know I want to make love with you and I'm not sure you're ready to take that step with me."

When she didn't respond, he brushed his lips across hers. "Are you, Rebecca?" he asked her softly. "Are you ready to take that next step and share my bed with me? If you did, I'd want to make love with you. I'd start by kissing you here." He drew back far enough to place a finger over the crease of her lips. With his gaze on hers, monitoring her response, he dragged the finger slowly over her chin, down her throat. "And here."

Shivers chased down Rebecca's spine as he dipped his finger into the hollow at the base of her throat. She felt the thundering of her pulse, and was sure he must feel it, too. But before she could will it to slow, before she could get a grip on her swirling emotions, he was sliding his finger down her chest until it rested in the valley between her breasts. Her skin burned where he touched her, her breasts ached for him to touch her there, as well.

He lowered his face over hers. "We'd make love for hours and hours," he said, his voice growing husky. "Until one or both of us cried for mercy."

He touched his lips to hers, and it was like touching

a match to dry tinder, the taste he brought to her the headiest of wines. Inflamed by one and drunk on the other, she wound her arms around his neck and held his face to hers. At her urging, he deepened the kiss, and she strained against him, desperate for him to relieve the throbbing ache in her breasts.

He obliged, slipping his hands between their bodies, his touch that of a master as he opened his palms over the swells. He squeezed, and hot arrows of desire shot to her center, leaving her weak and trembling. Wanting to experience more of him, to taste more of him, she combed her fingers through his hair, fisted them in the longer lengths at his neck and parted her lips beneath his.

Again he obliged and slipped his tongue inside. The sensual sweep of his tongue over hers was like an aphrodisiac, dulling her mind to all but the feel of his body pressed against hers, the gentle kneading of his hands on her breasts, the desire that swirled low in her belly.

A sound swelled inside her and rose to push against his lips, ripe with need, resonant with longing.

"The house," he murmured. He stooped and caught her behind her knees and swung her up into his arms. "I want you in my bed."

Rebecca buried her face against the side of his neck, her body burning with need. She clung to him as he strode to the house, and silently prayed that she could go through with this. She'd never wanted any man, any *thing,* as badly as she wanted Rob at that moment.

When he reached the bedroom, he lowered her to his bed and followed her down, finding her lips with his again. She opened for him, and with a groan he stretched out over her and stabbed his tongue deeply into her mouth.

His weight only added to the sensations already churning inside her, the pressure of his thigh against her feminine mound the most exquisite pleasure she'd ever known. And when he pulled his mouth from hers and lifted his head to look down at her, the heat in his eyes touched her soul.

His gaze never once wavered from hers as he reached for the buttons of her blouse. "Hours," he said huskily as he worked each disk free. "I'm going to make love with you for hours and hours and hours." He pushed aside the front panels of her blouse, sighed, then unhooked the front closure of her bra with a deftness she would wonder about later. "Days," he groaned as he freed her breasts and lowered his face over them.

She sucked in a breath when his lips first touched her flesh, held it in her lungs as he swept his tongue over an aching peak, then released it on a low, guttural moan when he opened his mouth over her completely and drew her in. The warmth of his breath set her nerve ends dancing beneath her skin. The rasp of his tongue across her nipple drove her mad.

But it was the greediness of his suckling that had her remembering the joy to be had in making love with a man, the thrill, the intense satisfaction derived in both giving and receiving pleasure.

She pushed at his chest. "I want to touch you," she told him, and rolled him to his back. Rising to her knees at his side, she reached for his shirt. "I want to feel the heat of your flesh on mine." Rob ripped open the fly to his jeans and shed them along with his underwear. She fumbled open the buttons, shoved the shirt over his shoulders…then sank back on her heels, awed by the masculine beauty of his sun-kissed skin, the obvious strength in the hardened muscles that lay beneath.

With a hum of delight, she placed her hands on his chest, mesmerized by the smooth texture of his skin, the difference in tone from hers; his stained a light cocoa by the sun, hers shades lighter. She spread her fingers wide, as if to measure the breadth, and felt the jump of muscle as her fingers bumped over his nipples.

Surprised by her ability to excite him so easily, and emboldened by it, as well, she shifted to straddle him and leaned to press her lips to his. When he tried to take possession of the kiss, to tug her hips up higher, she drew back. Although she wanted him inside her, as badly as he seemed to want her, she needed time more. Time to know him. Time to become familiar with him. His body. Time to make certain she had the courage to go through with this.

"No," she told him, and inched backward, her knees rubbing sensually against his thighs. "I want to please you first."

Rob wanted to stop her. Even reached out to grab her and tug her back. But then she touched her tongue to the tip of his sex, and his arms fell weakly to his sides, the strength drained from them. She slicked it around the head, circled it slowly, and he tensed, his body drawn as taut as a stretched bow, his hands fisted in the bedcovers.

Her aggressiveness shocked him, stunned him. Was this the same woman who had gone ballistic over a simple kiss? he wondered. But then she opened her mouth over him and took him in, her mouth a warm, moist glove around his length, and he lost all thought. All reason. All sense of time. His mind clouded with need, his body quaked with it.

Even as he silently prayed that she'd never stop, he

knew he had to put an end to this before she drove him over the edge.

Rearing up, he hooked an arm around her waist and dragged her back down over him. He closed his mouth over hers, silencing her protests, then rolled and forced her beneath him. All but blinded by lust, he curled his fingers in the waist of her slacks and jerked, sending the button that secured them flying to bounce off the opposite wall. Her slacks followed closely behind.

He rose to his knees and tore off his shirt, tossed it aside. "I want you," he said, his voice raw with need, his eyes on fire with it. "Now," he warned. "Now."

And then he was stretching out over her, his flesh grazing hers, until he found her mouth again. While he kissed her, he raced his hands over her body, across her face, down her shoulders, along her sides, tracing her shape, her features, setting her nerve endings on fire. She writhed beneath him, a silent plea for him to ease the ache that threatened to consume her.

Sensing her urgency, he linked his fingers with hers and dragged her hands above her head. Held them there as he thrust his tongue deeply into her mouth. Curled his fingers tighter around hers as he pressed the hardened length of his erection against her center.

For Rebecca, the depth of his passion was incredible, unbelievable. Thrilling.

Overpowering.

Smothering.

Threatening.

The panic slipped up on her so quickly, she was caught unawares. One minute she was making love with Rob, his body a welcome weight on hers, his hands those of a clever sculptor as he molded and remolded her flesh to meet his. His taste a seductive nectar she knew she would never lose her thirst for.

The next, it was Earl's body that covered hers, a dead oppressive weight, pinning her down. It was Earl's hands gripping hers, holding her rigid while he forced her lips to part beneath his. Earl's tongue stabbing deeply and vilely into her mouth, choking her. Earl's knee wedged between hers, prying her legs apart. Earl who shoved his sex forcefully against her center.

In her mind she screamed for him to stop, begged him to release her. But she knew Earl would ignore her pleas. He'd never listened to her before. He would rape her, abuse her body and her mind, as he'd done so many times during their marriage.

But she wouldn't allow him to steal her soul, she told herself. Her soul was all she had left.

She squeezed her eyes shut against the humiliation of it all, the shame, and willed the tension from her body, from her mind. She wouldn't fight him, she promised herself. Not this time. Fighting Earl only made things worse, increased his thrill, the pain he inflicted. She would feel nothing. Nothing. She'd numb her body to his touch, dull her mind to whatever degradations he forced upon her.

Rob sensed the change in Rebecca immediately. It was as if she'd melted beneath him. Become boneless. Her fingers falling lax between his. Her lips motionless. Her body limp. Deathlike.

He drew back to look at her and saw that her eyes were closed, her face slack as if in sleep. ''Rebecca?''

He watched a tear leak from the corner of her eye, slide down her temple and plunk against the pillow. But she didn't move. Didn't make a sound.

Frightened by her almost comatose state, he grabbed

her shoulders. "Rebecca! What's wrong?" His blood chilled when her head lolled back lifelessly. "Dammit, Rebecca!" he shouted, shaking her. "Talk to me! Tell me what's wrong!"

He released her, his breath ragged, and opened his hands to look at them, fearing that in his impatience to have her, he'd hurt her in some way. His gut clenched in dread and he looked back at her…and saw her move. But only enough to turn onto her side and draw her knees to her chin. Her shoulders shook in silent, heart-breaking sobs.

Rob stared, his heart pounding wildly within his chest, goose bumps rising on his flesh. *God! What had happened? What had he done? What—*

No, he told himself, reining in the panic. He hadn't done anything wrong. He hadn't hurt her. This wasn't his doing. It was Rebecca's…or rather her past's. A flashback, he told himself. She must have experienced some kind of flashback.

Knowing how he handled the situation was impor-tant, crucial even to her successfully overcoming what-ever atrocities she'd endured, he eased down behind her and curled his body protectively around hers. Careful to keep his movements slow, nonthreatening, he laid an arm in the curve of her waist and his head on the pillow next to hers.

He held her for what seemed like hours, gradually increasing the pressure of his arm around her waist until he had her tucked snugly in the curve of his body and against his chest. Her entire body trembled like a leaf.

"Rebecca?" he whispered close to her ear. "Baby, it's okay. Everything's all right now. I've got you. Rob," he added, wanting to make sure she made the distinction between him and whatever man had put this kind of fear in her. "It's me. Rob."

He repeated the same words over and over and over, until his voice was hoarse, his throat raw, unsure if she heard him, but unwilling to stop until she did.

The voice slowly penetrated Rebecca's mind, as if coming to her through a thick fog, cutting its way through the protective shield she'd built around herself. Masculine. Taut with worry. Husky, as it soothed. Muscle by muscle, her body relaxed, responding to the tenderness, the concern in the voice. Gradually she became aware of the body curved around hers, the strength in it, the protective cocoon it provided.

And then she remembered.

Rob.

It was Rob's body curled around hers, Rob's arms that held her close. Rob's voice that whispered soothingly at her ear. Shame flooded through her, pushing a fresh wave of tears to her eyes. He must think she was crazy. Mentally unbalanced. A sexual basket case. Twice now he'd attempted intimacy and both times she'd flipped out. Oh, God, she thought tearfully. How humiliating.

She had to get up, she told herself. She had to go home. She couldn't bear to see the pity in his eyes or, worse, the revulsion she might find there.

Carefully she began to move away from him.

Rob sensed her withdrawal immediately and tightened his arm around her waist. "Are you okay now?" he asked quietly.

"Y-yes. I'm...I'm sorry."

He heard the tears in her voice and pushed up to one elbow to look down at her. "You have nothing to be sorry about."

She squeezed her eyes shut, as if she couldn't bear to look at him—or was it that she couldn't bear for him to see her? He watched a tear leak from the corner of her eye to streak across the bridge of her nose. "Hey," he murmured, and turned her to gather her into his arms. "There's no need to cry. Everything's okay now."

She shook her head, her head bumping his chin. "It's just so embarrassing," she sobbed brokenly.

He hauled himself to a sitting position, pulling her up to cradle at his side. "What's embarrassing?"

Furiously she pushed away from him. "Me!" she cried, stabbing a thumb at her chest, then pushed her arm out to include the bed, the situation. "This! You must think I'm crazy. Deranged! A sexual cripple."

He caught her before she could roll from the bed, and dragged her back against his side. "No," he said, and wrapped his arm around her waist to hold her there. "I don't think that at all."

Unable to break free from him, she bent forward and buried her face in her hands. "Well, you should," she wailed miserably, "because I am."

"You're not."

She snapped up her head to glare at him. "How would you know? You hardly know me."

"I know enough to know you've been abused."

The blood drained from her face.

"Why don't you tell me about him, Rebecca?" he said quietly. "Tell me who hurt you?"

He watched the tears spill over her lower lashes, the slow fall of her chin to her chest. He sensed her embarrassment, her shame, understood it, and wanted desperately to free her of it.

He took her hands in his. "Rebecca. I want to help you."

She shook her head. "You can't. Nobody can."

"I can if you'll let me. Talk to me. Tell me what happened. If not about your past, then tell me what happened just now. Why you froze up on me."

Seven

Rob waited a heartbeat. Two. Three. Sure she wasn't going to answer. When she did, it was in a voice so low he had to strain to hear her.

"I haven't always been this way."

She looked so fragile, so broken, sitting there, her head bowed, her shoulders sagged in defeat. He wanted to tell her to forget it, that it wasn't necessary for her to tell him about her past, that it was wrong of him to ask her. More, he wanted to gather her into his arms and just hold her, until all the ugly memories were purged from her mind.

But before he could do either, she dragged her hands from his.

"I used to enjoy sex," she said quietly. She opened and closed her hands on her thighs, staring at them, as if transfixed. "Once. A long time ago. Then, it was beautiful, exciting, a sensual blending of bodies and minds. It was never painful. Never humiliating. Never forced or ugly. But that was before…before he—'' She pressed her lips together and shook her head, her eyes filling again. "I—I'm sorry. I…I can't talk about this."

He covered her hands with his. "Don't, then. Forget the past. Just tell me about now. What just happened."

Rebecca swallowed, gulping back the tears, knowing he deserved at least that much from her, after she'd all but come apart in front of him. Yet she wondered if he realized how closely the two were intertwined. "I…I panicked. Like the other time. When you kissed me. Before, you had me pushed up against the wall. This time I was pinned beneath you. Both times I thought you were…" She curled her hands into fists beneath his. "I thought you were someone else. I thought you were going to hurt me."

A tear rolled down her cheek and he brushed a knuckle across the dampness, catching it before it could fall. "I'd never hurt you, Rebecca. I've told you that."

She bobbed her head. "I know," she replied in a voice thick with tears. "I do. But my mind plays these tricks on me. The situation. A feeling." She shook her head. "I don't know how to explain it. But something happens that clicks a memory, and I think it's him, that he's got me. That he's going to hurt me again."

"Who, Rebecca?" he asked gently. "Who's going to hurt you?"

She lifted her face, her lips trembling, her eyes flooded with tears. "Earl. My husband."

A band tightened around Rob's chest at the anguish in her eyes, the fear that lay a thin layer beneath it. Unable to bear to see her suffer any longer, he gathered her into his arms. "He can't hurt you anymore, Rebecca. He's gone. Earl's dead."

"I know," she said, hiccuping a sob. "But he still has the power to control me."

"No, he doesn't."

She jerked away from him so fast, she was out of his arms before he could react.

"He does!" she cried. "Don't you see? He's *here,* in my head, all the time, controlling me. I'll never be normal again. Nothing will. I can't even have *sex* without freaking out!"

"Yes, you can."

She dug her fists into her thighs. "I can't! Don't you understand? Didn't you see what just happened?"

"Yes, and I understand perfectly. But I know how we can overcome your fears."

She stared at him a full minute, her chest heaving, her hands still clenched into fists. Then, slowly, she unfurled her fingers. "How?" she whispered.

Rob rose to his knees and pulled her to her knees to face him. With his gaze on hers, he slid his arms around her waist. "Look at me. If you're able to do nothing else, keep your eyes on me."

Though she did as he requested, he felt the rigidness of her body, saw the doubt begin to slide back to shadow her eyes. Without moving his gaze from hers, he opened his palms on her back and stroked slowly up and down. "You can do this, Rebecca. You can. I'll help you. Hold on to me, if you want."

She inhaled deeply, and lifted her hands to his shoulders.

Her touch was light, tentative. Her eyes swirled with conflicting emotions. Hope. Fear. Doubt.

"You're a beautiful woman, Rebecca," he said softly.

She dropped her gaze, her cheeks flaming. "I'm not."

He drew a hand from around her to force her chin back up. "Who told you that? Earl?" Before she could answer, he said, "You *are* beautiful. Don't ever allow anyone to try to convince you differently." He slid his arm around her waist again. "Uh-uh," he warned when she started to lower her gaze. "Your eyes are on me. Remember?"

Though reluctant, she complied.

Touched by her trust in him, her determination to see this through to the end, he pressed a kiss to her forehead. "Do you know how irresistible I find you?" he asked, looking down at her. "How unbelievably sexy? I only have to look at you to become aroused."

She pushed at his shoulders impatiently. "Oh, please. There's no need for you to lie."

He tightened his hold on her, preventing her from twisting away, then took one of her hands and pushed it down his abdomen. Her eyes shot wide when she encountered his arousal. "See?" he told her. "I wasn't lying. I was telling you the truth."

He watched her throat convulse, then felt the tentative curl of her fingers around his sex. It was all he could do to remain upright. Her touch was sweetness. Innocence. Torture of the most pleasurable kind.

"Yeah," he murmured huskily as her fingers trembled down his length. He lowered his face to hers. "Just like that."

He kissed her deeply, passionately, then forced himself to draw back, not wanting to push her too fast. She needed slow. Patience. He'd give her both. "Doing okay so far?"

Her breathing ragged, she wet her lips and nodded.

"Good." He slid his hands down her back as he leaned to brush her mouth with his again. "You've got a nice butt," he murmured against her lips. He cupped her cheeks and squeezed. "Just the right size. And your breasts—" He eased back and dipped his head down, opening his mouth over a peak. He flicked his tongue over a nipple, drew her deeply in, suckled a moment. He hummed his approval low in his throat as he pulled away. "Perfect." He lifted his gaze to hers. "You. In every way."

Tears flooded Rebecca's eyes. But this time not from shame or fear or anger. These tears were spawned by Rob's kindness, his tenderness. His understanding.

It was then that she began to believe that he really could help her, that he was capable of wiping from her mind all the ugly memories Earl had left her with. She began to believe, really believe, that he could heal her. That she could have sex with a man, this man, without breaking down.

Praying that was true, she opened her hands on his chest, over his heart. "I'm not perfect," she said, her voice breaking. "No one is. But thank you."

She watched the blue in his eyes soften, a tender smile curve his lips. He lifted her hand from his chest and placed a kiss in the center of her palm. "Maybe not, but you're damn close." He pressed another kiss against her palm, then lifted her hands to wind them around his neck. "Remember," he said. "Keep your eyes open and on mine." With that last reminder, he settled his hands in the curve of her waist.

Holding her steady with nothing but the power of his gaze, he took his hands on a journey downward, smoothing them over her hips, down her thighs, his touch like silk sliding sensually over her skin. Light. Hypnotizing in its slow, studied movements down, then up again, curving his hands until only the tips of his fingers brushed the inside of her thighs. By the time he reached the juncture of her thighs, his palms drawn together almost prayerfully at her mound, her body trembled with need, all but burned with it. Her eyelids grew heavier and heavier, her breath shorter.

He slipped a hand between her legs. "No, Rebecca," he whispered when her eyelids shuttered closed. "Look at me."

She managed to force her lids up, her gaze to his. But with each stroke of his finger along her feminine folds, her ability to keep them open grew weaker and weaker, as did her knees. And when he separated the folds and pressed the tip of his finger to her damp center, she dropped her head to his shoulder with a moan.

"Look at me, Rebecca," he ordered. "Look at me."

Though she wanted only to feel, to float on the sensations that he had sent pulsating through her body like waves against a distant shore, she dragged her head up, her eyes open.

Blue struck blue when their gazes met again. Heat pulsed against heat. With her arms wrapped tightly around his neck she clung to him, trembling, as he circled her center, gathering the moistness, spiking the heat...then suddenly he pushed inside. She gasped, arching, as he held her there, as if balanced on a high pinnacle, her body convulsing wildly.

Rob watched the surprise widen her eyes, the passion darken them, the flush of it stain her cheeks. Heard the pleasure, the satisfaction in the moan that slipped past her lips.

"Rob," he told her, wanting to cement his name in her mind, and hopefully tie it to the emotions she was experiencing. "Rob," he said again as he eased her down to the sheets and stretched out over her.

With his gaze fixed on hers, he held himself above her as he aligned his sex with hers. "Rob," he said yet again, then pushed inside her. She bucked wildly against him, her feminine walls clamping tightly around his sex. His arms trembled as he fought for control. "Rob," he repeated through clenched teeth as he drove his hips against hers again and again and again.

The tension built inside him, became a roar in his ears, a whip that lashed through his body, and he knew it was useless to try to hold back any longer. With a low growl he thrust deeply one last time and emptied his seed inside her. He jerked once reflexively. Again. A third time. Then, with a moan, he collapsed against her and buried his face in the curve of her neck, his energy spent.

"Rob," he groaned at her ear. He wrapped his arms around her and rolled to his back, bringing her with him. With a hand cupped at the back of her neck, he drew her head to rest against his. "Rob," he murmured, and turned his lips against her cheek.

He closed his eyes, surrounded by the scent of their lovemaking, comforted by the warmth of her body nestled against his, and whispered one last time.

"Rob."

Hours and hours and hours, he'd promised her.

Rebecca discovered Rob was a man of his word.

Snugged against his back, she lifted her head to peer at the bedroom window. An inky darkness shadowed the landscape beyond and a cycle of moon hung from a midnight-blue velvet sky. She glanced at the bedside clock and sighed. Almost eleven. She should go home. She leaned to peek over Rob's shoulder. In sleep, his face was relaxed, almost boyish. No scowling frowns to detract from his handsomeness now.

Though she wanted to lie back down and sleep curled beside him, she knew she had to go home. But leaving was difficult. Especially when he looked so adorably rumpled, with his hair all mussed and his jaw shadowed by dark stubble. Unable to resist, she bent to press her lips against his cheek, then shifted away from him to push from the bed.

A hand closed around her wrist and yanked her back. Shrieking, she fell across his broad back, her face only inches from his.

"Don't go," he murmured sleepily. "Stay."

Her heart melted at the huskiness in his voice. Smiling softly, she swept a hand across his forehead and brushed the rumpled locks of hair from his face. "I have to. Sadie. She's been in the house by herself all day."

"You put out food and water, didn't you?"

"Yes."

He reached behind him, caught her hip and dragged her from his back to lie opposite him. Snuggling close, he nuzzled his face between her breasts. "Stay."

She felt herself weakening, but stiffened her resolve. "I can't, really. She'll be lonely."

He heaved a weary sigh, then rolled to his back and from the bed.

She sat up, staring, as he pushed one leg, then the other into his jeans. "Where are you going?"

He glanced her way as he pulled up his zipper. "To get Sadie."

* * *

In the end, they'd both gone to Rebecca's house to collect Sadie, as well as a change of clothes for Rebecca.

Though she might have expected to feel awkward spending the night with a man for the first time, she was pleased to discover that she didn't. Rob was an easy man to be around, comfortable in his body...and fascinated with hers.

"What?" she asked, catching him watching her again while she was preparing their breakfast.

"Nothing. Just enjoying the view."

She bit back a smile and gestured with the spatula at the window. "The best view is out there."

He pushed from the bar and moved to stand behind her, wrapping his arms around her waist. Nuzzling his nose at her ear, he ran his hands over her abdomen. "Not to me." He cupped them over her mound and squeezed. "The best view is right here."

Rebecca released a shuddery breath. "If you're hungry, you better cut that out. Otherwise, I'm liable to burn your pancakes."

His lips curved in a smile against her neck. "You can always make some more."

"Rob—"

He turned her in his arms and closed his mouth over hers, silencing her. She melted against him on a sigh, the pancakes forgotten.

The phone rang shrilly. Once. Twice. On the third ring Rob snatched it from the base on the wall beside him. Dragging his lips from Rebecca's, he pulled the phone to his ear. "Rob Cole," he said into the receiver.

When Rebecca tried to ease from his embrace, he tightened his arm around her, holding her firmly against his groin. She watched his forehead pleat in a frown as he listened.

"Okay," he said slowly. "Is he there?"

Wondering who he was talking to and what the person had said that would put that dark scowl on his face, she placed her hands on his chest, over his heart, and soothed him.

He glanced down at her. "Yeah," he said into the receiver. "I'll get there as soon as I can."

He returned the phone to its base, then settled his arm around her waist again.

"Bad news?" she asked hesitantly.

He flattened his lips and shook his head. "No. Not really. That was Seb's secretary. She was calling to tell me that they'd located Eric's computer."

"And Seb?" she asked.

He pulled his arms from around her and turned away. "She hasn't seen him. Nobody has."

Rob settled himself at the desk Sebastian's secretary had provided, and rubbed his hands together before positioning his fingers over the keyboard. "Okay," he muttered under his breath. "Let's you and me have a little talk."

He punched in codes and a screen appeared. One by one, he scrolled through the files listed, looking for anything suspicious, anything that appeared out of the ordinary. After an hour or more of scrolling and checking records, he pushed back the chair and tilted his head back, scrubbing wearily at his face.

Nothing, he thought in frustration. Zero. Nada. A bunch of charts and graphs. Nothing but a bunch of financial mumbo jumbo, exactly what he'd expect to find on a bean counter's computer.

Certain that there had to be more, praying he'd find *something* in the computer's memory that would lead him to Eric's murderer, Rob straightened and quickly typed in another series of commands, this time calling up Eric's e-mail software.

Starting with the most recent e-mails, those dated just prior to Eric's death, Rob began to scan through them. Within minutes, he was yawning.

"No wonder Sadie was the only female interested in the guy," he muttered disagreeably as he closed one post and opened another. The guy was a geek. A bore. Reading his e-mails would put Alan Greenspan to sleep. It was like trying to work your way through a thousand-page commentary on world economics, written by some professor with a zillion credentials after his name. No one-liners. No crude comments about some hot chick in receiving. No dirty jokes. No nothing. Just business, business and more boring business.

The next post that popped up had him tense and startled. He scanned quickly, then shifted his gaze back to the beginning and read through it a second time.

"Damn you, Eric! You're going to pay for this, you son of a bitch. That money deal was our secret. Ours! A deal that you stood to profit from the same as me. Well, you've blown it now, buddy. You'd better get your affairs in order, because your days are numbered. Get my meaning?"?

A cold sweat popped out on Rob's forehead. He clicked to open the file fully, in order to reveal the header. The date on the e-mail was three days prior to Eric's death. And the author?

Sebastian Wescott.

Rob shot up from the chair, sending it spinning crazily across the room. No, he cried silently, refusing to

believe the facts before him. Not Seb. Seb wouldn't
steal money from his own company. He wouldn't murder an innocent man. There had to be an explanation
for this. Someone had set Sebastian up. That was it. It
had to be. He'd talk to Seb, tell him what he'd found.
Together they could—

"Damn you, Seb!" he swore, remembering that he
didn't know where Seb was. And without Seb there to
explain all this, to help track down the real murderer,
Rob's hands were tied. He had no other options.

He had to take his findings to the police.

But first he had to see Rebecca, he told himself. Hold
her. Surround himself with her sweetness, her innocence, to draw from her the strength he needed to turn
over to the police the evidence that would incriminate
his best friend.

When he arrived at her shop, he was grateful to find
Rebecca alone. She glanced up at the sound of the
chime, a smile blooming on her face when she saw him.
But as she started around the counter to greet him, her
smile slowly faded.

"Rob? What's wrong?"

He grabbed her hand and dragged her after him into
the storeroom. He kicked the door closed behind them
and spun her around and into his arms. His mouth
slammed against hers with an urgency, a desperation
that stole her breath and gripped her heart, while his
arms threatened to squeeze her in two.

A day before, Rebecca would have panicked at the
anger she tasted in him. Would have cringed in fear at
the violence she sensed in the corded arms that bound
her. But that was before. And this was Rob. Not Earl.

A distinction between present and past Rob had sealed so securely in her mind and heart the night before.

So instead of shrinking away from him like a coward, she leaned into him, wound her arms around his neck and opened for him, offering freely whatever he wanted to take from her.

And when she did, his mouth softened on hers, his hands opened to slide down her back. He moaned against her lips, the sound that of a wounded animal, and Rebecca absorbed the sound, wanting to take away whatever pained him.

When at last he withdrew, he did so on a ragged sigh. He rested his forehead against hers. "I needed that. You."

Touched more than he would ever know by his words, she cupped a hand behind his head and tipped her face up to kiss his chin. "Are you okay?"

He unwound her hands from his neck and held them as he took a step back. He gave them a squeeze. "I am now."

At that moment, as she looked into the depths of his blue eyes and saw the agony he suffered, glimpsed the pureness and tenderness of his tortured soul, Rebecca knew her heart was lost to him. "Tell me what's happened."

He did, explaining in detail the e-mail he'd found on Eric's computer, the implications of it, the ramifications it would have on Seb when Rob turned it over to the police.

"Do you think he's guilty?" Rebecca asked hesitantly.

He shook his head. "No way. But that e-mail says otherwise, and it's probably enough to send Seb to prison."

"Then don't do it."

Rob lifted a brow. "Don't give the police the e-mail?" At her nod, he turned away, cuffing a hand at the base of his neck and squeezing. "I have to," he muttered. "I don't have a choice."

"I'm not saying you should never turn it over to the police. I'm just suggesting that you wait a day or two."

He glanced over his shoulder at her. "And hope in the meantime that Seb shows up?"

"Yes."

"It's against the law to withhold evidence."

"I know."

"I could go to jail, probably lose my investigator's license."

Rebecca inhaled deeply, knowing how much Rob would be sacrificing if he were wrong about his friend. He stood to lose his career, his reputation. Possibly years of his life locked in a cell. And she would lose, too. She'd lose Rob. And she'd only just begun to believe that there might possibly be a future for them together.

She released the breath slowly, carefully, then crossed to him and took his hands in hers. "Or you might save a friend's life."

Rob stared at her, stunned by her belief in him, her faith that he was right about Seb.

"You don't know anything about that e-mail," he warned her. "I never mentioned it to you. Understand?"

She looked at him in confusion. "What?"

"You don't know anything about the e-mail," he repeated, gripping her hands tightly in his. "I never told you about it. This conversation never occurred. You're never to mention this to anyone. If you do, and the police get wind of it, then you will be as guilty of with-holding evidence as I'm going to be."

Rebecca told no one about the e-mail Rob had found. It wasn't a hardship, though. There really wasn't anyone she normally confided in. Other than Andrea, of course. But she didn't tell Andrea. Instead she worried…especially about Rob's safety.

He was dealing with a murderer, after all. If it wasn't Sebastian, who Rob was convinced was innocent, then that meant there was someone else out there, lurking about. Someone who knew about the e-mail, who had planted it in Eric's files himself, in order to frame Seb and hide his own guilt. There was a murderer walking around free, a murderer who would consider himself safe once Seb was accused of the crime and arrested.

A murderer Rob would bring to justice…or possibly die trying.

Haunted by that thought, Rebecca forced herself to stay busy, focusing her attention on the project for Rob's home when there were no customers to occupy her mind. She made an appointment for the next after-noon to discuss the final design of the koi pond and patio fountain with the contractor she'd selected for the job.

And worried about Rob.

She placed the special order for the bent willow fur-niture for his porch from a craftsman she knew in Mis-souri.

And worried about Rob.

And when five o'clock came and Andrea breezed into her shop, inviting her to join her for dinner at Claire's, the French restaurant on Main Street, she accepted, grateful for the distraction.

Once they were seated at the restaurant, Andrea braced her arms on the table and leaned forward expectantly. "All right. Let's have it. Tell me everything."

Horrified that Andrea somehow knew that Rob had sworn her to secrecy, Rebecca stammered, "Th-there's nothing to tell."

Andrea dismissed her evasion with a flap of her hand. "There is, and we're not leaving this restaurant until you tell me every gory detail."

While Rebecca stared, her stomach knotting in dread, Andrea sank back smugly in her chair. "I dropped by your house last night."

"I—I'm sorry I missed you. I wasn't home."

"I know. I called several times, too."

Rebecca couldn't think how to reply. She hated to lie. Andrea was her friend. But the thought of telling her that she'd spent the night with Rob... Wasn't that the same as kiss and tell? "Did you get my machine?" she asked, hedging.

"Yes. And you really should change your message. You must've had a cold or something when you recorded it, because you sound all nasal."

"I did have a cold," Rebecca said, leaping on the opportunity to distract Andrea. "Remember? It was about a month or so ago. You brought over chicken soup."

"Yeah. I'm a real Girl Scout. Now, about last night. Where were you?"

Rebecca could feel the heat crawling up her neck. "I worked late."

"I drove by the shop. Your van wasn't there."

"I wasn't at the shop."

"For heaven's sake, Rebecca, why don't you just tell

me that you spent the night with Rob, instead of making me drag the story from you?''

The heat made it to Rebecca's cheeks and burned.

Andrea leaned across the table, her eyes dancing with amusement. ''That good, huh?''

Rebecca rolled her eyes. ''Andrea. Please.''

''Am I embarrassing you? Sorry. But I'm not giving up until you tell me every last detail.''

The waitress arrived to take their orders, and Rebecca breathed a sigh of relief, grateful for the reprieve.

It was a short one.

''So?'' Andrea said as she handed their menus to the waitress.

Rebecca watched the waitress cross back to the kitchen, wishing she could go with her.

''Re-bec-ca,'' Andrea said, enunciating each syllable.

Wincing, Rebecca unfolded her napkin and spread it across her lap, knowing it was useless to hedge any longer. Andrea would get the story out of her one way or another. ''Yes, I spent the night at Rob's, and, yes, we…'' She felt the color rising again, and said in a rush, ''And, yes, we made love.''

''Woo-hoo!'' Andrea shouted as she sank back in her chair, applauding. ''I knew you could do it.''

Mortified that some of the other guests in the restaurant might have overheard their conversation, Rebecca glanced around before snapping, ''Andrea! Get a grip, would you? I'd just as soon the whole town isn't privy to my sex life.''

Andrea pursed her lips, trying not to laugh. ''Oh, but it's such an exciting one. Especially after such a long dry spell.''

Rebecca arched a brow in warning.

Andrea pushed a hand at Rebecca. ''Oh, all right,''

she groused. "Not another word, I promise." She picked up her glass, took a sip, set it down, opened her napkin, spread it over her lap, sat back in her chair and drummed her fingers on its arms, then puckered her lips as if whistling a silent tune.

And all the while looked everywhere but at Rebecca.

"Oh, for goodness sakes," Rebecca complained. "If you'll stop acting like a two-year-old, I'll tell you."

Andrea leaned forward, all ears.

And Rebecca told her. Stretching the story out over their salads, through their main course and ending it with their last bites of chocolate crepes.

Andrea laid down her fork, her eyes dreamy. "How romantic," she said with a sigh.

"Hello, ladies."

Rebecca glanced up to find Rob and Keith Owens, the owner of a computer software firm, approaching their table.

She gave Andrea a kick under the table. "Don't you dare let on that you know anything," she warned, then looked up to smile at Rob. "Hi. We just finished our dinner."

Biting back a grin, Rob stooped and thumbed a smudge of chocolate from the corner of her mouth before touching his lips to hers. "So I see."

Blushing, Rebecca stole a glance at Andrea as she dabbed at her mouth, fearing Andrea would make some comment about the kiss. She was relieved when she saw that Andrea was watching Keith Owens and had missed the whole thing.

Rob looked from Keith to Andrea, then pulled out Rebecca's chair. "Since you're all done," he said, "I'll give you a ride home."

"But I have my van," she said, balking, as he tugged her to her feet.

"We can get it later." He slid the strap of her purse over her shoulder, then cupped her elbow. "Nice to see you, Andrea," he said, then turned to Keith. "Later, buddy."

"But I haven't paid for my dinner," she protested, digging in her heels.

Rob pulled a fifty from his pocket and dropped it on the tray of a passing waiter. "This should cover the tab for that table," he said, indicating the table where Andrea still sat.

They were out of the restaurant and in his car before Rebecca had a chance to take a breath. "What was *that* all about?" she said indignantly as Rob slid behind the wheel.

He started the engine, then adjusted his rearview mirror. "You didn't notice?"

"Notice *what?* The only thing *I* noticed was you hustling me out of the restaurant before I could even say goodbye to Andrea."

"Hustling?" He chuckled. "I thought hustle meant to flirt with someone."

"It means forcing someone to go somewhere they don't want to go."

"You don't wan't to be with me?"

She folded her arms over her chest. "Don't try to distract me. I want to know what that was all about."

"Oh. That." He leaned over and dropped a kiss on her pursed lips and laughed when she drew back, narrowing an eye at him. "*That* was about Keith and Andrea. They were making moon eyes at each other. I figured I'd give him the room to make a move on her, if he wanted."

She dropped her arms, her mouth sagging open. "Keith and Andrea?"

He pulled away from the curb and eased into traffic. "Yep. Keith and Andrea. They were an item a few years back. While in college. Looked to me as if they could be again."

"Keith and Andrea?" she said again, unable to imagine the two together. "Why, she's so easygoing and friendly, and he's so…so…"

"Driven?" Rob suggested.

"That's putting it mildly."

He lifted a shoulder. "They say opposites attract."

Only just aware that he was heading for his ranch and not her house, Rebecca turned to look at him. "Where are you going?"

"Home."

"But—"

"You're going with me."

Rebecca kept up her arguments as she trailed Rob into his house.

"But I need to go home. I don't have a change of clothes."

He tossed his briefcase onto the kitchen counter. "You can wear some of mine."

"Not to work in the morning! What would people think?"

He opened the refrigerator and stuck his head inside. "Don't go to work."

Frowning, Rebecca slapped her arms together at her waist. "I *have* to go to work. I'm the owner."

He straightened, twisting the cap off a beer. "If you're the owner, then declare tomorrow a holiday."

He tipped the beer toward her, offering her a sip, and she shoved it away.

"I can't just close the store."

"Why not?"

"Because my customers depend on me, that's why."

He took a swig, then gestured at her with the bottle. "So what happens when you're sick?"

"I go to work anyway."

"What if you were real sick? Too sick to go to work? So sick you couldn't get out of bed?"

She frowned, never having considered the possibility, as she was rarely ever ill. "Well, I guess I'd have to stay home."

He slung an arm around her shoulders. "You know," he said, walking with her toward his bedroom, "you're not looking so good. Do you feel all right?"

"I feel fine."

"I don't know," he said, eyeing her doubtfully. He stopped at the side of his bed and pressed a palm to her forehead. "You feel pretty warm to me. You might have a fever."

She rolled her eyes. "I feel fine."

He set his beer on the bedside table and stripped back the covers. "Maybe you should rest for a while. Just in case."

"I'm not resting. I feel fine."

"You'll feel better once you get those clothes off and get under the covers." He reached for the top button of her blouse. "Here. Let me help you."

"Rob!" She swatted at his hands, but he'd already managed to undo two, exposing a sizable expanse of bare skin.

"What is that?" he asked, pleating his brow in concern. "A rash?"

Rebecca craned her neck, trying to see. "Where?"

"Here." He touched a finger to the middle of her chest, then dragged it down and hooked it in her bra. He yanked her to him. "Gotcha."

Rebecca huffed a breath. "You're a rat."

"And you're cheese. Rats love cheese." Grinning, he nibbled his way up her neck.

By the time he reached her ear, Rebecca would have been willing to be anything he wanted her to be. "Rob?"

He nuzzled her ear. "Hmm."

"You could've just asked."

"And ruin all the fun?"

"Whose fun?"

Laughing, he fell back on the bed, taking her with him. "Mine."

Eight

Still grinning, Rob ran his hands down her back and squeezed her rear end. "Damn, you've got a nice butt."

Rebecca toyed with a button on his shirt, unsure if she was ready to forgive him yet for tricking her into his bed. "If you have a fondness for such things, I suppose I do."

He hooted a laugh. "I do believe we're making progress. The woman almost accepted a compliment."

Softening, in spite of her determination to hold on to her indignation a little longer, she tipped her head to the side. "Almost?" she challenged, then pushed to sit up, straddling him. "Then please allow me to clarify." She reached for the top button of her blouse. "Yes, I do have a nice butt," she said as she slowly freed each disk. "And what's more I have really nice breasts." She peeled off her blouse and tossed it aside. "Not too big..." She unhooked the front closure of her bra.

"And not too small." She peeled one strap slowly down an arm, then the other. "As Goldilocks was prone to say, 'They're ju-u-st right.'"

Rob swallowed hard, staring at her bared breasts. He remembered her saying that she used to enjoy sex, and during their previous night's mating he'd seen glimmers of a more aggressive side to this woman. But he'd had no idea that she could be so playful...such a tease.

He wondered what other surprises she had in store for him, what other parts of her personality her former husband had suppressed that would begin to surface now he'd convinced her that Earl no longer had the power to control her.

The thought of her former husband and the abuse Rebecca had suffered at his hand shot anger through his system. No, he told himself, forcing the rage back. She'd seen enough anger, had lived with it far too long. He reached for her, wanting to show her once again that passion and pain weren't always synonymous. "Let me see if they taste as good as they look."

Cupping her breasts, she melted down on a sigh, offering them to him. He swept his tongue across a nipple, moistening the tip, shifted to wet the other. Then, shaping his hands over the outermost swells of both breasts, he brought them together and looked up at her. "Beautiful," he murmured, before he opened his mouth over both tips and drew them in.

Twin spears of desire shot through Rebecca, coming together to pierce her low in her belly. She arched at the sharp, sweet stab, pushing her breasts against his face, greedy for more, offering him more. His tongue and mouth were a blend of torture and pleasure, sensations that she'd willingly have endured for hours.

But she wanted to give, not take. To please, not hoard

all the pleasure for herself. Anxious to share all he'd given to her, she rose. "My turn," she told him as she wriggled out of her slacks. She tossed them aside, then inched back to sit on his thighs.

With her gaze on his, she spread her hands over his abdomen, a sensual smile curving her lips. "You have beautiful skin," she whispered. "So dark. Smooth as silk." She leaned to open her mouth over a spot just above his naval. She blew, warming his skin, then flicked her tongue at the moisture she'd left there before slowly straightening. She drew a circle in the moisture as she returned her gaze to his, her smile growing at the passion she saw staining his cheeks, darkening his eyes. Emboldened, she fanned her hands out, then up, smoothing them over his ribs.

"And muscular," she murmured. "Silk stretched over iron." Her fingertips bumped over a ridge of softer flesh and she drew back to peer at the place. A thick rope of scar tissue lay between two ribs midway up his right side. Frowning, she traced the length of the scar, then glanced up at him. "How did you do this?"

He caught her hand and drew her down. "Clumsy. I fell."

Before she could ask more, he closed his mouth over hers and caught her hips, drawing her higher up his body. "You weaken me," he said against her mouth. He nipped at her lower lip, then sighed against them. "And make me feel like Superman at the same time."

She shifted, making herself more comfortable. "Do I? That's odd, because you seem to have the same effect on me."

He brushed the hair back from her face to look at her. "That's not all you do to me." He reached between them and drew his sex between her spread legs. The blue in his eyes darkened, sharpened. "You make me hard, needy. You could make me beg, if you wanted."

Stunned that he'd confess to such a weakness, yet at the same time humbled by the trust displayed in sharing it with her, she pushed her hips down. "Never," she promised as she took him in. "I want only to please you, never control."

He lifted his hands to push his fingers through her hair, held them there, his gaze burning into hers. "Then please me now."

He raised his hips, even as she lowered hers...and the pleasure began. His legs tensed with it with each rhythmic thrust, hers quivered with it with each tortured withdrawal. The pace increased gradually, pushed faster by their increasing desire to please the other. The heat burned higher, hotter, became desperate, until perspiration slicked their skins and dampened the sheets.

He rolled, penning her beneath him. "I want you. All of you."

And all was what Rebecca wanted to give him. Her body, her heart, her soul. She didn't fear losing a part of herself in the giving. Unlike Earl, Rob would never take what she offered and abuse it. He would never tear at her, stripping away pieces of her personality and confidence until only threads of her true self remained.

She wove her fingers behind his neck and drew his face to hers. "I'm yours," she whispered. "All of me."

With his gaze locked on hers, he gripped his hands over the edge of the mattress and pushed hard inside her, held himself there. The muscles in his arms corded at the effort, his body trembled with it. She gasped, the intensity of his passion almost too much for her, the need for her own release too great...then slowly she came apart beneath him, a shattering of emotions that swept her up high and fast. She clung to him, her body joined to his at their most intimate centers, her heart thundering in unison with his.

For that single, precious moment in time, she felt she was part of him. One with him. She knew his thoughts. Shared his heartbeat. Experienced his joy, his pain, his sorrows as if they were her own.

Love.

Her heart swelled with it, her throat tightened with it. She knew that, at last, she'd found the man she could love, the man who would love and respect her in return.

While Rob slept, Rebecca watched him. She was too wired to sleep.

She was falling in love, and the feeling was too new, too exciting, too exhilarating for her to even think about rest. She wanted to dance on the ceiling, scream the news from the rooftop, run naked through the pastures.

She pressed her mouth to his shoulder to smother a laugh. Imagine. Her, Rebecca Todman, even *thinking* about running naked outside.

But she would. Could. She felt that free, that bold.

She rested her chin on his shoulder and stared at his profile. So handsome, she thought with a sudden rush of emotion. So tough, yet so kind. She'd known him less than two weeks, yet she didn't question her feelings for him. She didn't know what forces of nature had brought her to Royal and to Rob. But she did know that this was the man she'd dreamed of. The man whose image she'd clung to in order to survive the hell she'd lived in.

For a moment she let herself remember her life before moving to Royal. Her marriage to Earl. The two-year courtship. Their wedding. The shock when she'd discovered his darker side. The fear, the pain that had followed. She'd wanted so badly to leave Earl, to escape it all. But he'd controlled more than her body—he'd controlled her mind. He'd mentally beaten her down until she believed him when he told her that she was lucky to have him. That the beatings were all her fault. She believed him, too, when he'd told her that no other man would ever want her. That she was stupid, helpless, frigid and so on and so on, until he'd totally destroyed her self-confidence, her belief in herself as a woman.

A tear slipped from the corner of her eye and dropped to Rob's shoulder. She swept a thumb across it, smearing it.

But that was the past, she told herself, closing off the memories. She wasn't stupid or helpless. She'd proven that to herself by striking out on her own, leaving Dallas and moving to Royal. And she'd built a business for herself, a good one, and without anyone's help.

And she wasn't frigid, either, she added as she snuggled behind Rob again. With his help, she'd proven that to herself, as well.

Sleepy now, she laid her head on the pillow beside his and molded her body to his curves. With an arm curled at his waist, she closed her eyes.

And slept.

"Why do you have to go to work?"

"I've already told you," Rebecca replied patiently as she placed their breakfast dishes in the dishwasher. "I have a business to run. People depend on me."

"And one measly day off is going to put a bankruptcy sign on your door?"

She laughed at the little-boy pout in his voice and

dropped a kiss on his lips as she swept past him. "I don't want to chance it."

Scowling, he bent and scooped Sadie from the floor and followed, stroking the cat's back. "But you're coming back here after you close. Right?"

She sat down on the edge of the bed to put on her shoes. "Right. I'm meeting the contractor here at five-thirty." She stood and held out her arms. "Come on, Sadie. It's time for us to go."

Rob turned, hunching a shoulder and preventing her from taking the cat. "She can go with me."

"Are you sure?"

"Yeah," he muttered. "I need somebody to ride shotgun."

Fear twisted her nerves at the reminder of the danger he might possibly be placing himself in, and she moved to slip her arms around his waist. "Are you going to look for Seb?"

"Yeah. Got to. If the police find out about that e-mail before he surfaces…"

She rose to her toes to kiss him, knowing as well as he what that would mean. "Just be careful. Okay?"

"Always."

Dorian lifted his hands. "I haven't seen him. Nobody's seen him. Frankly, I'm worried."

With Sadie curled on his lap, nibbling at the pretzel Rob held for her, Rob studied Dorian from across the table, while Will Bradford, Jason Windover and Keith Owens listened intently to what Seb's half brother had to say. Though Dorian and Seb shared some physical characteristics—the same chestnut-brown hair and unique silver-gray eyes—for Rob the similarities ended there. There was something about Dorian that bothered him. He couldn't put a finger on exactly what it was, but something about the guy disturbed him, and had from the moment Seb had introduced his half brother to the members of the Cattleman's Club and asked that he be allowed to join the exclusive club. Out of friendship to Seb, Rob had agreed.

Dorian glanced at the cat, his disgust obvious. "I thought only Seeing Eye dogs were allowed inside the club."

Rob stroked a hand along Sadie's sleek back. "They made an exception, since she's riding shotgun for me today."

Rolling his eyes, Dorian pushed back from his chair. "Riding shotgun," he muttered. "You'd think you were a Texas Ranger or something."

"Next best thing," Jason said proudly, slapping Rob on the back. "Both always get their man."

Dorian snorted, then lifted a hand in farewell. "I've got to get back to work. See you guys later." As he passed Rob's chair, Dorian leaned to pat Sadie on the head, but yanked his hand back when the cat hissed at him.

"Crazy cat," he muttered as he stalked away.

"Whose cat is that, anyway?" Keith asked.

Rob kept an eye narrowed on Dorian's back, watching him leave. "Eric Chambers's."

"Chambers's?" Jason echoed. "What are you doing with his cat?"

Rob watched Dorian disappear beyond the door, then turned to look at Keith. "Rebecca's keeping him until Eric's next of kin is located." He lifted a shoulder and stroked a hand over the cat's back. "I'm just baby-sitting, while she's at the shop."

William Bradford lifted a brow in surprise. "I didn't know you were seeing Rebecca Todman."

Uncomfortable hearing the association, Rob squirmed in his chair. "I'm not seeing her exactly."

Keith howled a laugh. "Could have fooled me. You should have seen the lip-locker he put on her at Claire's last night," he said to William. "Right there in front of God and everybody."

Rob shot him a murderous look. "I'm surprised you noticed, since your eyes were glued on Andrea."

"Andrea O'Rourke?" William repeated.

It was Keith's turn to squirm. He dismissed Rob's comment with a grunt. "He's just trying to shift the heat to me. He's *gone,*" he said, indicating Rob. "The woman's got him wrapped. Hell, she's even got him baby-sitting her cat. Next thing you know, she'll be dragging him down the aisle. Then it'll just be me, Seb and Jason left to choose the charity for the Cattleman's Ball."

Rob's hand froze midstroke on Sadie's back, his body tensed in denial. "No way," he said, shaking his head. "Rebecca and I are just…friends."

Keith stared at him in amazement. "Are you kidding me? I've seen the way she looks at you. The lady's as gone for you as you are for her. Mark my words," he warned. "Your days as a bachelor are numbered."

"We want three, maybe four boulders stacked about here," Rebecca said to the contractor, indicating the spot in the atrium where she wanted them placed.

"And the fountain concealed inside 'em?" the contractor asked.

"Yes."

"What about the mechanical equipment? It's got to go somewhere."

She pursed her lips, considering. "I guess you could place it in the far corner there, build a box around it, then conceal it with more rock." Rebecca turned to look at Rob, who stood before the great room's rear window, staring out. "Rob? Is that all right with you?"

When he didn't respond, she sighed and turned back to the contractor. "Conceal it in a box." She glanced around, then lifted her hands. "I guess that about covers everything, unless you have any questions."

He tugged on his cap, then tucked his clipboard under his arm. "No, ma'am. I've got all the information I need."

Rebecca followed him to the door. "When can you start?"

"Day after tomorrow, if that's okay with you. I've got a couple of days' break in my schedule then, before I'm to start my next job."

"Perfect. Then, I'll plan to see you here at eight in the morning, then."

After closing the door behind him, she returned to the great room and crossed to stand behind Rob. "Hey," she said softly as she slipped her arms around his waist from behind. "What's wrong?"

He lifted a shoulder. "Nothing."

She turned her cheek against his back and rubbed. "Something is. You haven't said two words since you walked in the door."

He pulled away from her and cupped a hand at the back of his neck as he moved away.

Rebecca stared after him, stung by his rejection. "Rob? What's wrong?"

"I told you. Nothing's wrong."

But something was wrong, she could feel it. "Is it Seb? Did you find him?"

"No."

"Any word on where he might have gone?"

"No."

Hearing the frustration in his voice, she moved toward him. "If you're worried about him—"

"I said it's nothing," he snapped.

"Something's bothering you," she insisted. But before she could demand that he tell her what it was, he swore, then bolted for the back door.

"Rob!" she cried. "What is it? Where are you going?"

"It's Seb!"

"Sebastian?" She ran after him. "Where?"

"I just saw him drive by." He jerked open the door and started out, but turned, blocking her way, when Rebecca started to follow. "Wait inside. What I have to say to him won't be fit for a lady's ears."

Hugging her arms around her waist, Rebecca moved to the window to look out. Sure enough, it was Sebastian who stepped from the car parked on the driveway behind Rob's. Rob stopped him before he reached the house.

Rebecca didn't have to hear their conversation to know that what Rob had told her was true. What he had to say to his friend was definitely not fit for a lady's ears. Body language alone told her that. Rob squared off, his legs braced, his hands bunched into fists at his sides, as if preparing for a fight. She couldn't see Rob's face, only Sebastian's, and his was a study of...blankness. There wasn't a sign of emotion on his face. No anger. No remorse. Nothing.

She could hear Rob's raised voice, but couldn't make

out his words. She watched him gesture wildly, then give Sebastian a shove. Sebastian stumbled back a step, but made no move to defend himself. Rob shoved him again. Again. Still Sebastian did nothing.

Then Rob dropped his arms to his sides, his shoulders sagging in defeat. He said something to Sebastian— what it was she didn't know, and the man replied. A short response. No more than a couple of words. Then Sebastian turned, opened the door to his car and slid behind the wheel.

Rebecca heard the sound of the engine start. Saw the expression on his face as he turned to look up at Rob. Grim resolve? Fear? Before she could decide, he reversed, turned and drove away.

Rob stood on the driveway staring after him until the car disappeared from sight, then slowly turned and walked back to the house. Rebecca met him at the door.

She saw the defeat in the slump of his shoulders, the concern that creased his brow, and she opened her arms to him. "Oh, Rob," she murmured sadly, wanting to comfort.

He pushed past her, and yanked his shirt over his head. Rebecca stared after him, again feeling the sting of rejection. A bubble of fear rose and she forced it back, determined not to allow him to intimidate her with his silence, as Earl had often done. She was equally determined he wasn't going to ignore her.

She followed him as he strode for the bedroom.

"Rob, talk to me. Tell me what's wrong. What's happening."

He jerked a fresh shirt from the closet and slammed the door. "Nothing. I told you. Nothing's wrong."

He turned his back to her as he tore the shirt from the hanger. As he did, she caught a glimpse of the scar again. That raised ridge of tissue that lay between his ribs. On his back she saw another scar, this one flat, a fine, thin line paler than the rest of his skin. Another peeked from the waist of his jeans, snaking along his spine, as he shrugged on the shirt.

Before, when she'd asked him about the scar at his ribs, he'd told her he'd fallen, was clumsy. Now she wondered if he'd lied. Rob wasn't clumsy—he was athletic, as surefooted as a deer. She couldn't imagine him any differently as a child.

So why had he lied?

She crossed to him and watched his shoulders tense as she neared. Steeling herself for another rejection, she lifted the tail of his shirt and pushed it up his back. She traced a fingertip lightly along the scar, and felt him stiffen even more. Tears pushed at her throat as Andrea's words whirled around and around her mind, making her dizzy, making her ill.

...carried a bull whip with him all the time...some said he even slept with it...jerked the trainer down from the horse...took the bull whip to the animal...vet said he'd never seen such a bloody mess...

Bloody mess...

Bloody mess...

Bloody mess...

She closed her eyes, gulping. She could see Rob as a young boy, knobby knees, gangly arms, skinny as a rail. His thin chest and back tanned by the sun, his shoulder blades poking out from his back as sharply as elbows. She could see him cowering away from his father. Hear the vicious *crack* of the whip. Feel the pain as it lashed across his back, opening flesh beneath it. Hear his screams.

She gulped again, and forced her eyes open to stare at the scar. "He did this to you. Your father."

He stepped away, yanking the shirt from her hand and quickly buttoning it.

But it was too late. She'd already seen the damage. Already put the missing pieces of the puzzle together. Now she understood why he had known, without her first telling him, about her abusive past. Why he'd seemed so callous, so emotionally aloof when she'd first met him. He'd known she'd been abused because he'd been abused himself. And he was callous, aloof because he'd learned the hard way not to trust...especially those who claimed to love him.

Yet, even knowing what he faced, he hadn't run from Rebecca's insecurities and hysterics, as another man might have done. No, he'd stuck by her, even helped her come to terms with the atrocities of her past, offering her both his understanding and his comfort.

But as he stood across the room from her, his back as rigid as a wall of impenetrable steel, she sensed he wouldn't welcome her comfort, would resent any words of sympathy she might offer.

So she gave him her heart instead.

"I love you."

He flinched as if she'd struck him. "No," he said, shaking his head. "You can't."

"I know my own heart. I love you."

He continued to shake his head, as if in doing so, he could keep her words, her love from touching him.

"You can't," he said. "I don't want you to love me."

Furious with him, she snapped, "Well, that's too bad. I can't change my feelings. They're there. So deal with them."

He whirled then, his nostrils flaring. With his gaze fixed angrily on hers, he tore open his shirt, sending buttons flying, exposing his chest, the scar that lay between his ribs. "You asked me how I got this and I told you I fell. It wasn't a lie. Not entirely. I fell, all right. I fell while running from my father."

"The whip," she said, her eyes filling.

"So you've heard about my old man."

"A little. I asked Andrea about him. But she never told me that he'd abused you."

"Abused?" He dropped his head back and laughed, though the sound lacked any trace of amusement. "Such a safe, polite little word. I'm surprised that you, of all people, would use it. Why don't you call it what it is? Hell. Sheer hell. My father didn't *abuse* me, Rebecca. He beat me. Then beat me some more, if I cried.

"He was my father. And because he was, he knew my every weakness. My every fear. And he capitalized on them. I hated spiders. Was terrified of them. So he locked me in the root cellar. No lights. No windows. Just darkness and dank earthen walls and floor. And spiders. Millions of them. They dropped from the ceiling onto my head, crawled up my legs, my arms, my face. I screamed for hours. Begged him to let me out. He did. The next morning. Sixteen hours he kept me locked in there. Sixteen hours of sheer hell."

At some point during his story, Rebecca had covered her mouth with her hands. She didn't remember raising them, didn't know which part of the horrible scene he described had triggered the reaction. A part of her wanted to cover her ears, as well.

But Rob wasn't through with his story. Not by a long shot.

"The perfect childhood," he said bitterly. "Every

kid's dream. But there were times I actually prayed that he'd put me in the cellar. I'd have preferred it to some of the other ways he found to terrorize me."

Unconsciously he rubbed a thumb over the scar on his rib, as if the wound still pained him. "The whip was bad. But it wasn't the worst. I had a dog. Rip. He went everywhere with me. My best friend. One day I found him hanging from a rafter in the barn, a noose around his neck. I didn't have to ask who'd killed him. I knew. After that I never dared let on that I cared for anything. A pet, a toy. Certainly never a human being." He shook his head. "If I had, I knew he would destroy it, just to hurt me. To see if he could make me cry."

Rebecca forced her hands from her mouth and drew in a shaky breath. "I don't know why you're telling me all this. If it's to try to change my feelings for you, you've failed. If anything, I love you even more, knowing what all you endured as a child, and the kind and generous man you are today, in spite of it."

He snorted and turned away. "Then you're a fool."

Rebecca had been called a fool before, even believed it for a time…but never again. No one would ever call her a fool again. She was across the room, had him by his arm and was spinning him around, before he knew she'd even moved.

Her voice shook with fury, not fear, as she faced him. "If you consider me foolish for loving you, then so be it. But don't ever make the mistake of calling me a fool. I won't allow you or anyone else to ever call me that again."

She released his arm. "I don't know what you're trying to accomplish with this conversation, but I'll tell you this. Nothing you say will change what I feel for you. Nothing."

He lifted a brow. "Really? Try this. I beat my father so badly he was hospitalized for six weeks. Plastic surgeons had to rebuild parts of his face."

Stunned, she staggered back a step. "No," she whispered, and covered her ears with her hands, not wanting to hear any more. "You're lying."

"Oh, it's true, all right. Ask Andrea, if you don't believe me. I beat him with my bare hands. My hands," he repeated, and took a step toward her, lifting them, as if to show her the blood that stained them.

She stood her ground, refusing to let him bully her into fearing him. "If you did, it was self-defense. You're not a violent man."

"Aren't I?" His voice was flat, emotionless.

She slapped his hands from before her face, furious with him for trying to turn her heart against him. "No, you're not. But you're a coward. You're so afraid you'll be hurt again that you've chosen to feel nothing instead. You've built this huge wall around your heart, closed off all your emotions. And for what?" she demanded of him. "A life void of all emotion, all pain? A solitary life where you never have to fear anyone disappointing you again?"

"It's the choice I've made."

The tears came and she didn't even try to stop them. "Well, guess what, tough guy. Life is filled with pain. It's unavoidable. No matter how hard you try to safeguard yourself, it will find you." She took a step back from him, dragging a hand beneath her nose. "I know, because I thought when Earl died, I'd never hurt again. But you've hurt me. You never lifted a hand to me, yet you've hurt me more than he ever did. You've broken my heart."

Nine

Rob stood in the doorway of Seb's office, watching as a team of detectives from the police department conducted their search. Seb was there, too, though Rob wondered how he stood it. Having to silently watch while complete strangers dug through your business and personal files would be a hard thing for any man to swallow. Especially a man like Seb.

Though Rob had been hired by Seb to find Eric's murderer, he wasn't there in an official capacity. He was there as a friend. Seb's friend. As mad as he was at Seb for continuing to refuse to tell the police where he was the night Eric was murdered, Rob wouldn't let him suffer this indignity alone. He understood the reason for Seb's silence. The covert activities conducted by the members of the Texas Cattleman's Club sometimes required a need for secrecy that superseded civil law...and sometimes the member's own safety.

But knowing that didn't make it any easier for Rob to accept. He was worried about Seb, concerned that, in remaining silent, Seb was writing his own one-way ticket to prison. The night before, when Seb had stopped by his house, Rob had tried to reason with him, warn him what was at stake. When that hadn't worked, he'd considered just beating the hell out of him. But how could he fight a man who just stood there, stoically prepared to take whatever Rob wanted to dish out?

"Take a look at this."

His attention grabbed by the detective's request, Rob watched one of the detectives pass a file to another. The second man flipped through it, then shared a glance with the other.

Footsteps sounded behind Rob and he glanced over his shoulder to find a third officer entering the room. Without acknowledging Rob's or Seb's presence, he crossed to the two detectives and handed them a folded document. The two scanned it quickly, then rose to face Seb.

"Mr. Wescott," the one in charge began, "we have in our possession a warrant for your arrest. You have the right to remain silent. You have the—"

The roar in Rob's ears blanked out all other sound. *No,* his mind screamed. *No!*

He looked at Seb, silently begging him to say something, explain whatever it was the detectives had found. But Seb said nothing. Did nothing. Just stood, his expression giving away nothing, and listened to the detective quote him his rights.

But when one of the detectives pulled out cuffs, Rob couldn't take any more. He stepped between the man and Seb. "Allow the man some dignity. Don't make him walk out of here in cuffs."

The detective stared at Rob a long moment, then shifted his gaze to Seb. Scowling, he clipped the cuffs back to his belt. "Don't make me regret this," he muttered as he gripped Seb's elbow and ushered him through the door.

Rob didn't remember anything after watching Seb slide into the back seat of the police car. He knew he must have climbed into his own car and driven away. He surmised that much, because he was currently sitting in it. What he didn't know was how he came to be parked in front of Rebecca's house, or even how long he'd been sitting there.

It was dark now, and it hadn't been dark when the police had taken Seb away. The sun had been shining then. Rob knew, because he remembered wishing it would disappear behind a cloud or something. Anything to save Seb the shame of people seeing him being shoved into the back seat of the police car and driven away to jail.

He stared at Rebecca's house, noting that no lights glowed in the windows, and asked himself, *Why here?* Why had he driven to her house? Why had he sought her out, when the previous evening he'd done everything he could possibly do to run her off?

He didn't want her to love him. Hell, he didn't even believe in the word, the emotion. And why should he? Every person he'd ever loved had disappointed him. As a young boy, he'd loved his father and what had that gotten him? Beatings, cruelties beyond belief. He'd loved his mother, too, and had watched her turn her head away when his father would whip him. He'd believed her when she would cry later and tell him that if he'd only be a good boy, his father wouldn't have to whip him. It wasn't until he was grown and his mother was dead that he was able to forgive her for not protecting him, to understand she'd truly believed that if he were good, his father wouldn't beat him. It had taken maturity and the ability to look back before he'd understood that she was a victim as much as he, that his father's abuse hadn't been reserved just for Rob. He'd abused Rob's mother, as well.

As he stared at Rebecca's house, the urge to go inside was so strong, he had to grip the wheel to keep from giving in to it. More than anything, he wanted to hold her. To surround himself with her sweetness, her innocence...her love. He wanted to bury himself inside her and forget the look on Seb's face as the police car had driven away. He wanted to forget his father's cruelties, his mother's weakness.

He just wanted to be with her.

But he couldn't allow himself to give in to the urge. To do so would be feeding the weakness, losing, little by little, the strength that had helped him survive.

To do so would be opening himself up for pain again, disappointment. If he went to her, she'd see his weakness, know how much he needed her and loved her. She'd use his weakness to hurt him, disappoint him. She'd turn it and twist it, until he was that young boy again, cowering and begging beneath the lash of the whip.

No, he told himself, and jerked the car into gear. He was better off alone.

Alone, there was no pain.

There was nothing.

Blessed nothing.

Rebecca glanced up at the sound of the chime.

"Have you heard anything?" Andrea asked as she

hurried to the counter.

Startled by Andrea's stricken look, Rebecca set aside the arrangement she was working on. "About what?"

"Sebastian Wescott. Didn't you know? He was arrested. The police think *he* killed Eric."

Rebecca sank onto the stool, suddenly too weak to stand. "Arrested?"

"Yes. Last night. Supposedly they searched his office and found some kind of document. Some kind of evidence that he was the one who killed Eric."

"The e-mail," Rebecca whispered, wondering if Rob, in the end, had decided to give the evidence to the police.

"I was hoping Rob would have told you the details. This is all so awful. So unbelievable."

Rebecca averted her gaze. "No. I haven't seen Rob." She plucked a flower from a bucket and forced herself to place it in the arrangement.

"Rebecca? What's wrong? Has something happened between you and Rob?"

Rebecca wouldn't look up. She couldn't. The hurt was too fresh, the rejection too sharp, for her to talk about it. "No. The project at his house is coming along nicely. In fact, I met the contractor there yesterday morning to begin work on the fountain in the rock garden."

Andrea rounded the counter. "I wasn't talking about the job. I was talking about the two of you. Your relationship."

Rebecca waved a careless hand. "There isn't a relationship. We're just friends. That's all. Nothing more."

Andrea caught her hand before Rebecca could draw another flower from the bucket. "That's bull, and you know it. You were more than friends. You were lovers. What happened?''

The tears surged to Rebecca's eyes before she could stop them. She lifted her gaze to Andrea's. ''Oh, God, it hurts so badly.''

Immediately sympathetic, Andrea draped an arm around her shoulders and headed Rebecca for the back room. ''I know,'' she soothed. ''Love usually does, at one time or another. Now tell me what happened. Maybe it's just a misunderstanding. Couples have them all the time.''

''No,'' Rebecca said, sniffing. ''There was no misunderstanding. Rob made his feelings known quite clearly. He doesn't want a relationship with me. Not ever. He even tried to turn me against him by telling me that he'd fought with his father and put him in the hospital.''

''He did fight with his father,'' Andrea said quietly, then added quickly, ''but it was self-defense. Rob found his father beating his mother and pulled him off her. They fought and—'' She lifted a hand helplessly. ''His father wound up in the hospital, nearly every bone in his face broken. No one blamed Rob, although there was an investigation. Everyone knew how mean Mr. Cole was. It was no secret.''

''You don't have to convince me of his innocence,'' Rebecca said as she pulled a tissue from a box and blotted her nose. ''I know Rob would never harm anyone, unless he had a very good reason. It's Rob who considers himself violent. Not me.''

Rob avoided the Cattleman's Club. He couldn't bear to even walk past the front door. When he did, he was

swamped with memories, regrets. He saw Seb everywhere he looked. Heard his voice. His laughter.

He should have been able to do something to prevent
this, he told himself furiously. He should have forced
Seb to tell the police where he was the night of Eric's
murder. He should have found that file before the police
did, and destroyed it. Buried it somewhere it would
never be found. Burned it!

But he hadn't done any of those things, and now one
of his best friends was behind bars.

As he led the mare out to the pasture, he found no
comfort in knowing that Seb alone was responsible for
his own imprisonment. There was nothing Rob could
have done to save his friend. Not when all the evidence
pointed to Seb's guilt.

But he's not guilty! Rob raged silently. That was the
rub. An innocent man was behind bars, while a murderer walked the streets, and there wasn't a damn thing
Rob could do about it. Not until Seb was willing to talk,
not until he was willing to help Rob prove his innocence. Three days now, and not a word from Seb. He
refused to see any visitors, refused to talk to anyone.
He seemed resigned to being accused of Eric's murder.

His steps weighted by the sense of helplessness he
carried, he released the horse in the pasture and trudged
back to the house. Once he was inside, the walls seemed
to close in on him. Everywhere he looked he saw signs
of Rebecca. The pots of herbs she'd placed in the
kitchen window. The twelve-foot pine that filled the
corner of the great room and stretched almost to the
ceiling. The debris scattered about the atrium, left there
by the contractor Rebecca had hired.

Unable to look at any of it, he strode to his office.
The message light on his answering machine blinked at

him from the corner of his desk. He hit Play, then propped a hip on his desk while the tape rewound.

"Rob? Rebecca Todman."

He tensed at the sound of her voice.

"I'm sorry, but I won't be able to complete the job we contracted for. I've dropped a check in the mail, to reimburse you for the deposit you made, less the expenses incurred to date. I—"

She paused, and he leaned forward expectantly, anxious to hear what else she had to say, desperate to hear the sound of her voice again.

"I'm...I'm sorry," she said, then there was a *click*.

He punched the replay button and listened to the message again. The sound of her voice was so crisp, so businesslike, so unlike the Rebecca he'd come to know...until the end. But he heard the misery in her "I'm sorry," felt the words wrap around his heart and squeeze.

I'm sorry.

He pushed to his feet and stood, his eyes burning, his throat on fire. And what did she have to be sorry for? he asked himself. What sin had she committed? Whom had she wronged?

Her only sin had been in giving too much, falling in love with the wrong man. And if any mistakes were made, they were made by Rob. He'd lost his focus for a moment, let down his guard.

And in the end, he'd hurt her.

But no more than he'd hurt himself.

It's best this way, he told himself, and headed for his room. For both of us. Cut your losses and move on, wasn't that what he'd learned? Wasn't that the philosophy he'd chosen to live by?

He stripped off his shirt and crawled beneath the covers, exhausted.

But sleep wouldn't come.

Her scent surrounded him, haunted him. That light, floral scent he'd learned to associate with her. He turned to his side…and could almost feel the warmth of her body curved behind his. He rolled to his back and fisted his hands over his eyes to block the memories.

But he could still see her. The sweetness of her smile. The passion that had darkened the blue in her eyes each time he'd filled her. Her voice echoed around him, husky, giving. *I'm yours. All of me.*

Furious that he couldn't escape her, he heaved himself from the bed. On his way to the patio, he grabbed a bottle of whiskey from the bar in the great room, then flopped down on a chair at the patio table, determined to drown the memories.

To forget.

To numb the pain.

Rebecca unlocked her back door and stepped inside her kitchen, exhausted after putting in a full day at her shop. "Hey, Sadie," she murmured wearily, scooping the cat up to nuzzle at her neck. "Did you miss me?"

"Yeah, as a matter of fact I did."

She jumped, startled, at the sound of the male voice, then slowly turned to find Rob standing before her sink, his hips braced against the counter, his arms folded across his chest, watching her.

She glanced at the door.

"Don't worry. You remembered to lock it."

She looked back at him. "Then how did you get in?"

He lifted a shoulder. "I'm a private eye. We have our ways."

Anger pulsed through her, replacing the surprise, the shock of seeing him again, and she reached for the phone. "That's breaking and entering. I'm calling the police."

He caught her hand before she could lift the receiver from the base. "No need to call the police," he said as he pulled the phone from her hand. "I'm not here to rob you."

"Well, that's certainly a relief," she said bitterly.

He replaced the phone, then turned.

Something about the way he looked at her frightened her, and she backed up a step. "What do you want?"

He gestured toward the table. Lined up across its top were potted plants in varying stages of demise. Wilted blooms, dry and curled leaves, branches bare of any vegetation at all.

"They're dying," he said simply.

Though it was in her nature to heal, to nurture, Rebecca forced herself to remain where she was. "I can see that."

"Can you save them?"

Rebecca remembered another instance when he'd asked her to save a plant. At the time, she'd sensed that he was asking her to save him, as well. She hadn't understood why he would need her help, or known from what he suffered.

But she did now. And she also knew that she'd already done everything she could to help him, to heal him. She'd given him all she'd had to give. She given him her heart, and he'd refused it, even bruised it.

She stooped to set Sadie on the floor. "Sorry. It's too late."

"Are you sure?"

Fearing if she looked at him, she'd weaken, she

crossed to the pantry and pulled down a can of cat food. "Quite sure."

"But you didn't even look at them. How can you be sure they're beyond help?"

She positioned the can on the electric opener and pressed the button, holding the can in place as it turned. "I don't need to look any closer. There's no hope for them."

She heard his footsteps on the tiled floor, the scrape of a ceramic pot across the table's surface.

"I think I see some life here," he said. "A little bit of green."

Firming her lips, she peeled back the top of the can and spooned the food into Sadie's bowl. "Then take them home and water them. Save them yourself."

"I can't. I've tried. My way doesn't work."

She closed her eyes against the huskiness in his voice, the obvious need. "I can't help you, Rob. I can't."

"What if we both tried to save it? Together. Think that would make a difference?"

She opened her eyes, blinked back tears. "Why are you doing this? Haven't you hurt me enough?"

She felt his hand light on her shoulder, and tensed beneath it.

"I need you, Rebecca," he said quietly. "More than you will ever know. I'm sorry I hurt you before. I never meant to. I'd never purposely hurt you. I was only trying to save us both some pain."

She spun to face him. "Save us from what pain?" she cried. "Loving each other? Caring for each other? You can't avoid pain, Rob. Where hearts are involved, there will always be pain, as well as joy."

"I know that now. I thought by ending our relationship, sending you away when I did, that I could keep myself from falling in love with you.'' He lifted a hand to brush a knuckle beneath her eye, catching a tear before it fell. "But it was too late, Rebecca. I was already in love with you.''

She hiccuped a sob, afraid to allow herself to believe that he meant it. "Be sure, Rob. Oh, God, please be sure. I don't think I could bear it if you broke my heart again.''

He slipped his hand around her neck. "I've never been so sure of anything in my life. I love you, Rebecca. I've never told a woman that before. Never felt for one what I feel for you. You make me feel whole, complete. For the first time since I can remember, I *feel*. You did that for me. You opened my heart by giving me yours. Let me give you mine.''

She searched his gaze and found only sincerity there...and love.

"Yes,'' she whispered. "Yes.''

He pulled her to him, holding her against his chest. "Rebecca,'' he murmured. He tipped her face up to his. She was surprised to see tears in his eyes. "You humble me.''

She laid a hand over his heart. "And you give me strength.''

He shook his head. "No. The strength was always there. I just helped you find it again.'' He touched his mouth to hers. "Marry me, Rebecca. I don't want to waste another day of my life without you with me.''

She wrapped her arms around his neck. "Neither do I.''

He kissed her then, deeply, giving her a taste of what awaited her, the love he had to give her.

"Tomorrow," he said, drawing away to look at her. "We'll get married tomorrow."

"Tomorrow!" she repeated in surprise. "We can't possibly get married that quickly."

"This weekend, then," he said, willing to compromise. "We can have the wedding at the Cattleman's Club. They can handle all the details. All we'll have to do is show up."

Rebecca eased from his embrace and turned to look out at her backyard and the flowers blooming there, remembering the dreams she'd planted among them. "No," she said softly, feeling the petals of her dreams opening in her heart. "We'll have the wedding here. At my house. In my garden."

He moved to stand behind her and slipped his arms around her waist. Resting his cheek against hers, he said, "Whatever you want. Whatever makes you happy."

She turned in his arms, smiling through the tears. "You make me happy, Rob Cole. Only you."

Epilogue

Rob hadn't had much experience with weddings. And certainly never one from the groom's perspective. But as far as he could tell, this one was just about perfect. He'd overheard some of the female guests whispering about how Rebecca's garden looked like something straight out of a fairy tale and wondering if she planned to add wedding consultations to the other services she already offered at In Bloom.

Though he wasn't a man much for frills, Rob had to agree with the ladies. Rebecca's garden *did* look like something taken from a book of fairy tales. There were flowers everywhere. In addition to those already growing in her garden, Rebecca had filled baskets and vases with hundreds of cut blooms from her shop and placed them throughout the yard. Tiny white lights roped the trunks of the trees and lined the patio's roofline, while another larger light, one that cast a glow much like the moon, was concealed within the greenery that draped the wisteria-covered archway. It was beneath that circle of silvery light that Rob had pledged to love, honor and protect Rebecca.

And he would, he promised himself. He'd never let anyone hurt Rebecca again.

"What are you doing way over here all by yourself?"

Rob glanced down as Rebecca slipped an arm around his waist.

Smiling, he draped an arm over her shoulders and hugged her to his side. "I was just thinking what a lucky man I am. A beautiful wife to share my life with, and a wonderful circle of friends—"

He stopped midsentence, unable to finish.

Rebecca tipped her head against his shoulder. "I know," she said sadly. "I miss Seb, too. I wish he were here."

Rob firmed his lips, struggling against the emotion that tightened his throat. "Yeah. Me, too. It just doesn't seem right without him."

Rebecca shifted to stand in front of him, and slipped her fingers beneath his lapels. "We'll celebrate again, when he's cleared."

Rob forced a smile for her benefit. "Yeah. And I'll let Seb pick up the tab, for being such a jerk and missing our wedding."

Laughing, Rebecca pushed to her toes to kiss him. "That'll teach him a lesson, I'm sure."

Rob drew her to his side, watching with her as their guests milled about, laughing and talking. He saw Dorian talking to Keith, and frowned. "I heard Dorian hired some hotshot defense lawyer to represent Seb."

"I heard that, too," Rebecca replied. "Susan Wysocki, I believe was her name.'' She glanced up at Rob. ''Do you think she can prove his innocence?''

Rob lifted a shoulder. ''If Seb's willing to help her, she can.'' Seeing the worry in her eyes, he caught her hand and drew her back toward the crowd, determined not to let anything spoil her wedding day.

''How long before you think we can gracefully blow this joint?'' he asked.

Laughing, Rebecca hugged his arm. ''I'll race you to your car.''

*   *   *   *   *

One

"Sebastian Wescott has been arrested."

The news spread through the Texas Cattleman's Club like a wildfire devouring prairie grasslands during a season of drought. Muted whispers set in motion beneath an array of mounted glassy-eyed animal heads grew in intensity until the gleaming Tiffany chandeliers overhead nearly shook from the force of its membership's outrage. It didn't take long for a select group to abandon games of poker and pool where enormous sums of money were at stake to make their way quietly into one of the tasteful private meeting rooms at the back of the club. Here behind closed doors, where the lingering odor of expensive cigars was less noticeable, discussions of the most serious nature took place.

A silver samovar with piping-hot coffee stood untouched beside a set of fine bone china embossed with the club's distinctive crest. Nothing less than hard liquor was warranted as the rumors resonated from room to spacious room in the nearly-one-hundred-year-old building. Members in this time-honored, elite institution were more than social acquaintances. Few would have guessed from its modest exterior that the club was actually a front for a prestigious social enclave working on covert missions. Placed in situations in which the members were often forced to rely on one another for their very lives, they considered themselves closer than actual blood brothers.

Word of Sebastian's disgrace hit everybody hard.

His own half brother, Dorian, appeared inconsolable as he related to the group the events leading up to Seb's arrest. It was no secret to anyone there that Dorian had been deeply worried about Sebastian for the past several weeks. His concern had been the topic of conversation on more than one occasion and had been so overdone that it had put some of the members off. The club was a place where they came to relax at the end of a stressful day, not to wallow in unsubstantiated gossip about one of their own.

Only, now it appeared Dorian's fears were not unfounded.

"If only there were some way of helping Sebastian without somehow jeopardizing the anonymity of the club," lamented William Bradford. As Sebastian's partner at Wescott Oil Enterprises, he was fiercely protective not just of the business they ran together but also of his old friend Jack Wescott's son.

"Sebastian says he was out of town on business the night Eric Chambers was murdered, but I understand he refuses to provide his attorney with an alibi," Dorian interjected, anxiety deeply etched on features that reminded everyone present of his half brother.

It was only at Sebastian's insistence that the members of the club had unanimously inducted Dorian a short time ago. As a full-fledged member, he was privy to the workings of their brotherhood, but he hadn't been there long enough to have knowledge of the details regarding the daring missions that sometimes called club members away for indeterminate lengths of time.

It was all Jason Windover, the retired CIA agent, could do to refrain from explaining to this ninny that Sebastian often used his business as a cover. He had been wary of Dorian from the start, and time, unfortunately, hadn't improved his first impression of the man. In fact, Jason had only reluctantly agreed to participate in Dorian's induction ceremony as a favor to Sebastian. Not wanting to endanger a friendship that spanned so many years, he had set aside his misgivings and gone along with his friend's request without giving voice to his qualms.

Jason supposed his suspicions stemmed from his background as a CIA agent. Looking at Dorian now, it was certainly hard to doubt the sincerity of his feelings.

"I say the least we can do is put up his bail," William Bradford suggested not bothering to clear up any misconceptions Dorian might have about his brother's whereabouts on the night in question. "It's best if no money from Wescott Oil Enterprises is involved, since those funds are under such intense scrutiny at the present."

Dorian gasped as William's intention dawned on him. "Are you suggesting that we somehow come up with half a million dollars in bail money between us?"

"Pocket change," exclaimed Keith Owens. As the owner of a computer-software firm, he didn't so much as blink at the amount mentioned. "Count me in."

"Me, too," Jason said. As rich as Midas, he would have given everything he owned to support his old friend.

When Dorian sputtered in disbelief at their overwhelming generosity, they assured him that no one was taking an actual risk with their money. No one among them believed Sebastian would forfeit bond by running out on them. For that matter, no one doubted his innocence.

Lamenting that he personally had little money to put up, Dorian told them all, "I wish there was more I could do. I wish I could have somehow convinced that hotheaded brother of mine not to try solving his problems all by himself. Well, you all know how he is—so worried about depending on others. He'd rather take matters into his own hands than accept help from calmer heads even when the situation demands it. Lately he's been more short-tempered and violent than usual. I swear if I didn't know better, I might be tempted to believe that—"

Dorian stopped in midsentence as if realizing that he might have said more than he intended. He had the grace to look ashamed.

"I apologize for rambling on like this," he told the men assembled in the room. "It's just that I've been so worried, I guess—"

Eager to put an end to the conversation, Jason interrupted and quickly changed the subject. "No apology necessary, Unfortunately there is one item of business that we can't continue to ignore. Considering that the organizer of our annual Cattleman's Club Charity Ball is under arrest, I think it best if we simply cancel this year's bash altogether."

No amount of alcohol could wash away the bad taste

that announcement left in everyone's mouth. Aside from the fact that some very worthy charity would be adversely affected by this vote, none of the men assembled wanted to tell their wives and sweethearts that they were responsible for canceling *the* event of the year. The number of places in Royal where designer evening gowns and diamonds were standard dress was limited, and the ladies were sure to be disappointed. It was a point not lost on William. As the first member of the five friends who had made the bet—to succumb to the allure of marriage, he didn't fancy the idea of breaking the news to his lovely new wife. After enduring a period of restricted confinement to keep her safe, Diana had really been looking forward to this year's ball. If nothing else, she hoped to allay her friends' worries by her presence.

"Heck of a way for Sebastian to avoid paying up on his bet," Keith volunteered, hoping to lighten the mood. Of all those present when Sebastian posed his now infamous bet about who would be the last bachelor standing at the ball in question, only three remained in the running.

"You would have lost, anyway," Jason told him. Recognized as the club's premier playboy, he had no plans of ever tying himself down.

The ensuing bantering lacked the usual lightheartedness. The thought of Sebastian behind bars put a definite damper on what had started out as a pleasant evening. Beyond posting bail as quickly as possible, there was little any of them could do to help their old friend besides pray.

Each did pray in his own private way, passing one by one beneath the iron-studded sign that hung over the entrance door. It proclaimed the Club's motto for all to see: Leadership, Justice and Peace. Men willing to risk their own lives to promote those ideals were at a loss as to how to help one of their own. Perhaps, as Jason mused, "Faith" would have to be added to that venerable old sign.

* * * * *

You are invited to enter the exclusive, masculine world of the...

Silhouette Desire's powerful miniseries features five wealthy Texas bachelors—all members of the state's most prestigious club—who set out to uncover a traitor in their midst... and discover their true loves!

THE MILLIONAIRE'S PREGNANT BRIDE
by Dixie Browning
February 2002 (SD #1420)

HER LONE STAR PROTECTOR
by Peggy Moreland
March 2002 (SD #1426)

TALL, DARK...AND FRAMED?
by Cathleen Galitz
April 2002 (SD #1433)

THE PLAYBOY MEETS HIS MATCH
by Sara Orwig
May 2002 (SD #1438)

THE BACHELOR TAKES A WIFE
by Jackie Merritt
June 2002 (SD #1444)

Available at your favorite retail outlet.

Where love comes alive™

presents

A brand-new miniseries about the Connellys of Chicago, a wealthy, powerful American family tied by blood to the royal family of the island kingdom of Altaria. They're wealthy, powerful and rocked by scandal, betrayal...and passion!

Look for a whole year of glamorous and utterly romantic tales in 2002:

January: **TALL, DARK & ROYAL by Leanne Banks**

February: **MATERNALLY YOURS by Kathie DeNosky**

March: **THE SHEIKH TAKES A BRIDE by Caroline Cross**

April: **THE SEAL'S SURRENDER by Maureen Child**

May: **PLAIN JANE & DOCTOR DAD by Kate Little**

June: **AND THE WINNER GETS...MARRIED! by Metsy Hingle**

July: **THE ROYAL & THE RUNAWAY BRIDE by Kathryn Jensen**

August: **HIS E-MAIL ORDER WIFE by Kristi Gold**

September: **THE SECRET BABY BOND by Cindy Gerard**

October: **CINDERELLA'S CONVENIENT HUSBAND by Katherine Garbera**

November: **EXPECTING...AND IN DANGER by Eileen Wilks**

December: **CHEROKEE MARRIAGE DARE by Sheri WhiteFeather**

Where love comes alive™

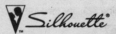